AF432976

Once In A Blue Moon

Book One: The Silver Crescent Witch

M. A. Ramsay-Scales

Cover art: Miblart
Chapter display photography: A.P.R.
Formatted in: Atticus

COMPLETED WORKS
Once In A Blue Moon

Dedications

I want to dedicate this book to my partner-in-crime, my husband and my best friend, my real-life Alpha.

I'm also dedicating this book to my Nana and Grampy; for always being there for me, encouraging me to step out of my comfort zone, and introducing me to my love of books.

I want to make a third special dedication to my two boys. Thank you for believing in your mommy and supporting me in accomplishing my dream. I only hope that accomplishing mine, helps you reach your own.

Dear Reader,

Thank you for your support in reading this book. You cannot know how much it means to me that you are taking a chance with me as an author. With that in mind, I do want to put a trigger warning letter here.

This book contains sensitive mature content that may be distressing or triggering to some readers and is not intended for audiences under the age of 18. Please be advised that the following themes are addressed in this book: sexual assault, drugs, alcohol, provocative language, explicit and sexual scenes, kidnapping, and murder.

I strongly urge readers who may be affected by these topics to exercise caution or consider if this material is suitable for their emotional well-being. If you find yourself becoming overwhelmed, I encourage you to reach out to a trusted individual or seek professional support.

Once again, thank you for your support.
Happy reading!
M. A. Ramsay-Scales

To women who have been abused, remember this: you are not
a victim, you're a survivor.
Know your worth and remember you are loved.

Playlist

GOOD AS HELL – LIZZO
SUPERMASSIVE BLACK HOLES – MUSE
RAISE HELL – DOROTHY
WHISPERS IN THE DARK – SKILLET
FIGHT SONG – RACHEL PLATTEN
CLOSER – NINE INCH NAILS
WITCHY WOMAN – EAGLES
POUR SOME SUGAR ON ME – DEF LEOPPARD
S&M – RHIANNA
ANOTHER LIFE – MOTIONLESS IN WHITE
CENTURIES – FALL OUT BOYS
LEVITATING – DUA LIPA
PRISONER – RAPHEL LAKE, AARON LEVY, DANIAL RYAN
MURPHY
ZOMBIE – DAMNED ANTHEM
COMATOSE – SKILLET
X AMOUNT OF WORDS – BLUE OCTOBER
PAIN – THREE DAYS GRACE
GIVES YOU HELL – THE ALL-AMERICAN REJECTS

A Glimpse into the World of Supers

IN A WORLD WHERE humans coexist, with supernatural beings, a delicate balance is maintained by a set of laws that govern their interactions. The laws have been molded to fit as society evolves, anyone who breaks the laws will face the Tribunal for sentencing.

The Tribunal, made up of a diverse group of supernatural beings, ensures adherence to these laws. They are the arbiters of justice, the enforcers of peace. May the Gods and Goddesses ever be in your favor. However, remember, in this world of supernaturals, it's not just about survival, it's about understanding and respecting the balance of power. There are only four laws that must be obeyed at all costs:

1. The woods and mountains are off-limits to vampires. Werewolves need nature and space to hunt animals and run free in their natural form. Vampires accept the risk if they enter without permission from the Alpha of the Silver Crescent Pack.

2. In return, Werewolves are to stay away from the Warehouse district. This area is strictly for Vampires and requires permission from the Queen of the Vampires for safe passage.

3. No fighting between any species. Humans are not to be used as cannon fodder or to be swayed into performing acts of violence for either side.

4. Dark Illusion is Switzerland during the full moon, meaning this is neutral territory. Both species may use the club to seek refuge so long as no blood is spilled.

Prologue

Roughly 1200 years before present day

BLOOD. BLOOD EVERYWHERE. AN innocent girl lays mangled on the cold ground; her face frozen in terror. I never should have done this. All I wanted to do was to save Nathan, my human lover. I never meant for the spell to get out of control the way it did and create a monster. My hands are coated in his blood, dripping, forming a puddle on the grass as my lover devours into the neck of the girl that I offered up as the human sacrifice needed for this spell. Nature requires a balance and there is always a price with magic. Especially dark magic. I just wanted to be with him for as long as possible.

"What have you done Melody?" I hear someone coming up behind me. I turn around slowly, my body trembling, silent tears developing at the disaster that has unfolded in front of me. I know what I have done is wrong. It goes against everything that I have been trained for as the future high priestess, but I just couldn't be without him. I look up and meet eyes with Chase, my werewolf lover and best friend. His face was dark, stern, and filled with anguish. He takes a step around me, examining the situation at hand. "Wha-what did you do?"

"I'm s-sorry Chase. I love you, but...." I stumble over my words, "I love him too. I-I love you both."

"This is unnatural, you have to kill it! You have to fix this. You're my mate, I will not share you with this abomination!" He demands. The noises that Nathan is making as he feeds, the crunching of limbs being ripped apart, the slurping, and growling, are unnatural; the noises that of an animal. Chase unbuckles his hunting knife from this belt, thrusting it into my hands. The weight of the knife feels abnormally heavy in my hand.

"This never would have happened if you hadn't killed him in the first place Chase!" I sob. It's true; Chase killed Nathan after my father ordered him to. My father is the Alpha of our pack, the Silver Crescent pack, and had arranged for Chase and me to be wed in a few moons from now. It's a big deal to be the daughter of the Alpha and to be married to the future Alpha, Chase. The problem is that I'm in love with Chase...and Nathan.

I've known Chase since my birth, we grew up together and our love blossomed and grew over time. When Chase turned 22, he and his wolf felt me as his mate, and he marked me as such that night.

I fell in love with Nathan, a local guy from the nearest town, a few months ago while running errands for my father. It felt like we had an instant connection, like a spark igniting. We talked for hours. After meeting Nathan, I started making excuses to run errands in town so that I could see him. Chase started to catch on and followed me one day, and like a good soldier and future Alpha, he reported his findings to my father.

My father confronted me about Nathan and gave me a choice. Leave Nathan or he dies. We tried to stay apart, but we just couldn't. So, my father gave Chase the order to protect our pack, to protect me as his mate, and to kill anyone who can't be trusted. With that choice, Nathan paid the price with his life.

I believed that this was the right thing, I truly did. Have you ever loved someone so much that you would do just about anything for them? Well, I did, and nature is going to make me pay for what I've done. It was my spell, my choice to go against nature...

I created a monster...a bloodthirsty monster.

My father called Nathan a **Vampire**...

One

Present Day

"ARE YOU EVEN OLD enough to be a nurse?"

Ugh...Sighs...

Looking down at the patient lying in bed in front of me, I'm just grateful for wearing a mask while on the hospital campus. Just another perk, or shall I say requirement, while living in a pandemic. It takes all my willpower to not roll my eyes when my patients question my skill level as a nurse.

"Yes, I am old enough to be a nurse," I reply as politely as I can. *If I told you how old I really was, you probably wouldn't believe me anyway.*

A different kind of perk of being a witch with werewolf traits. The patient just continues to glare at me, most likely doubting my statement, watching me go about my nursing duties and starting his IV infusion. He just stays silent, watching me with those eyes.

"Ok, if you need anything, you have your call light," I instruct him after getting the infusion set up and checking on the infusion pump and my patient one last time before I walk out the door and head back to my workstation.

My station is a mess, papers everywhere, and yet, I know exactly everything that is going on with my assigned patients. Flinging my mask off onto the desk and going through my report sheets, who do I go see next? Druggie, hernia repair, or dehy-dration?

Sighs.

"Another patient giving you a hard time again, Callie?" I peek over my monitor to see my coworker and mentor, Brody, giving me that look.

"I'm fine, really. Just another patient doubting my skills because of my looks." I smile and chuckle just a little.

"At least they aren't doubting you completely and asking if you are the nursing assistant," he retorts with a chuckle.

So very true. I can't imagine how hard it must be being a male nurse. I'm not a new nurse, I've been a nurse for years, and working here at this hospital for at least a decade. Brody, Brody Jameson, on the other hand, has been here since its creation in 1756.

Did I forget to mention that he's a vampire? He's one of the oldest people that I know and has truly been an amazing coworker, mentor, and friend. Oh, and did I fail to mention that he's gorgeous? He's one of those go-with-the-flow type of guys, down to earth and easy on the eyes of tall, dark, and handsome. He's also the world's biggest flirt and he doesn't do anything to hide who he is or his intentions. I think that is why I'm so glad that we got paired up during my orientation; he truly has been a lifesaver.

"Earth to Callie..." Brody calls over to me, waving his hand trying to get my attention.

"Sorry Brody, lost in my thoughts over here," I say wrinkling my nose before diving back into my work, researching the history of a couple of my patients. "What were you going on about?"

"I was asking if you were going to Dark Illusion tonight. I need a wingman, in this case, a wing-woman who can use her certain witchy powers to pick up on the sexy emotions," he states giving me a big smile like the Cheshire Cat.

"Hmm, I don't know Brody. Using my powers to help you get laid sounds like fun for only one of us." I tease.

Hmm...

Dark Illusion is the best club in this city and the only one that caters to the supernatural like me and Brody. It also happens to be one of the only few supernatural-friendly clubs within 100 miles, but only during the phases of the full moon. "You might just have to go this time without me. I've got plans that involve a stroll through the woods."

"You're the one missing out. Full moon is in the next couple of days. You know how intense the club gets during the full moon," He adds trying to convince me to reconsider. He's not wrong, the club is always filled with extra sizzle from the hormones of vampires, werewolves, and other supernaturals during a full moon. We are all affected by the full moon, not just werewolves like the myths and stories want you to believe.

"That's why I can't go Brody. I need to collect the herbs for all the orders for The Apothecary and other businesses in town." If I could go to the club, I would, but there are only a handful of witches who can make the elixir needed for those who don't have a safe place to go during the full moon.

During my days off I bake for a local cafe called The Apothecary, which has been in this city for as long as there have been supernaturals on earth. The list of customers gets longer and longer with each month; The Apothecary owner even fulfills online orders and ships out overnight, as the elixirs are only good for the three days of the full moon.

I peek over my computer screen to look at Brody, "You could always join us tonight for our stroll through the woods..."

"Us?"

"Yes, us. Forest and I are both heading out tonight after I get out of work. I don't know if you have seen the news lately, but with all the attacks happening, Forest is coming with me as protection," I add with a smile.

Silence.

Brody just stares at me with a raised eyebrow. "What?"

"Two things...First: why aren't you bringing Shadow? You would get more protection with your familiar. And second: You and Forest are spending a lot of time together recently, anything happening there?" He inquires.

"I AM bringing Shadow, strength in numbers. There is no way I would go into the woods without him. As for Forest, we are just friends. Safety in numbers, can't hurt to bring extra muscle." I can't help but blush though. I don't know what it is with the men in my life whether personal or professional, they are all gorgeous though.

"As much as I would love to join your rendezvous in the woods, you know I can't go. You will just have to survive with Shadow and Forest on your own." He goes back to his work. He's right, I have almost forgotten the rules; he isn't allowed to go into the woods at night, and no vampire is.

Supernaturals have been living in peace here in Capital City for centuries. The history I grew up with states that there was a war that was started between a werewolf, a mortal, and a witch. The witch fell in love with the werewolf and was betrothed. Later, she fell in love with a mortal, who the werewolf killed. The problem was that the witch brought the mortal back to the land of the living and created the first vampire. Not everyone knows the true story of how it all started, only those directly involved and their descendants. The war ended when the Queen of the Vampires, Alpha of the Wolves, and the High Priestess created laws for all supers to abide by and signed the treaty of peace in blood. That witch was my ancestor and was one of the most powerful witches of her day. I have been blessed, by the

Goddess and the Universe, to have been gifted with her powers as well and to have a wolf familiar.

Beep-beep...beep-beep...

Grrrrrr...groaning and rolling my eyes at my beeper. It only goes off if the ER requires my assistance and it's never good when they do. I look over at Brody, he gives me a sympathetic look. I read the page out loud "ED room 26 - SA victim. Needs SANE RN with powers STAT".

"That's all you kiddo," Brody chirps from behind his computer, "sounds like a doozy. Good luck!"

Sighs.

"Alright, I'm going. Cover my patients; here are my report sheets, they are all FULL CODES!" I snark with a smile. He takes my papers, nodding in agreement, adding them to his own. I grab my SANE backpack, filled with all my herbs and medical equipment that I could possibly need, and head to the ER.

***

I love my job; I love being a nurse... What I don't love is when this pager goes off.

SANE, Sexual Assault Nurse Examiner.

Now do you understand why I don't love it when my pager goes off, especially this close to a full moon? What's worse is that there are only a few SANE RN-witches around and only a couple employed with this hospital. It's just bad luck that a case came into the ER during my shift with the SANE pager.

At first glance, the ER at Capitol City Hospital is just like any other, a chaotic hornet's nest. Everyone is bustling around, talking over each other, providers needing medications to be administered or supplies, and nurses doing the best they can to keep the ship going. All with the goal to fix and heal patients while giving them the best care possible. I, unfortunately, knew the layout very well. There are about 3-4 cases of sexual assault that come through this ER every month. Sadly, it occurs so often, but it's part of my job and there are only so many nurses qualified to handle these cases, let alone powerful enough.

Looking around, there is only one nurse in the nurses' station, two active codes happening simultaneously, and every room is occupied.

Busy night, I guess.

"Did someone page for SANE?" I ask the only nurse in the station.

The nurse doesn't even have the courtesy to look up from her screen and replies, "Dr. Saunders did. He said for you to grab him before going on to see the victim. He's in the providers' lounge."

"Ok great, thank you," I say with a smile, walking away, heading towards the providers' lounge.

I try to be as polite as I can, I know that the ER nurses don't like having their department invaded by nurses who don't typically work with them. Hospitals are very "clicky", and it's not even a supernatural species thing either. Departments tend to stick together; it's just how it is. It takes a while to break the ice and to make friends or connections in other departments.

Finding Dr. Saunders, Dr. Galen Saunders, isn't hard to find in the providers' lounge, around the corner from the nurses' station. Taking a moment before going into the providers' lounge, I can see him dictating a note into a patient's chart. Instant heat floods throughout my whole body, because *daaaaamn,* that man is fine!

Standing height of 6'5", short dark hair, groomed and controlled facial hair, and dark eyes that can penetrate you in an instant; he's the standing definition of tall, dark, and deadly. I hate that he has this effect on me, not completely his fault though, being a werewolf and the Alpha of the Silver Crescent pack that claims this territory, just adds to his sexual appeal and Alpha aura.

Deep breath...time to be professional, I can drool later.

Knock-knock...

Opening the door and stepping into the providers' lounge is just so quiet. "Excuse me Dr Saunders, sorry to interrupt. You paged for SANE, but the nurse in the station said you wanted to see me first?"

Looking up from his monitor, and making eye contact, ignites my heat more. I quickly avert my gaze and adjust my kit, trying to be professional. There is a history between us, one that is hard to understand. We've known each other for years, he's a few years older. His family is close to mine, as in he took over as Alpha of the pack when my father stepped down. That's a long story for another day though. I owe him for finding me this job after completing my nursing degree and completing my SANE certification. We've been friends for years, and have come close to crossing the friend-zone line, but never fully crossed over.

"Ahh, yes, thank you, Callie. Let me get straight to the point..." He turns back to his screen to read me some basic pertinent information about the victim. "Female patient, approximately mid-20s, brought in via ambulance, friends called it in. Large party at Dark Illusion gone wrong. The patient is believed to be human, unconscious when EMTs arrived. By the time they got to the ER, the patient had become completely hysterical and combative. The patient is in active 4-point restraints due to self-harm and harm to staff." He sighs deeply, "Callie, she is a mess... We tried to give her sedatives to calm her down, but..."

"But what?" I ask with a hint of worry.

Normally, Dr. Saunders isn't this concerned or hard to read, "Whatever she ingested prior to partying at Dark Illusion is counteracting everything we've given her. She's been given enough to sedate an elephant. Nothing is working...I think she needs some magical intervention in order to give her the medical help she needs."

He looks back at me with those dark piercing eyes, "Which is why I paged you...personally. I think it would be best to take another set of hands in there with you, female only would be my guess. It's not pretty, this situation needs to be handled delicately."

He stands up and hands me the tablet with the victim's chart pulled up.

Taking the tablet from him, looking up at him as professionally as I can while gazing into his dark eyes, blushing "To be honest Dr. Saunders, I'll go in first alone and assess the situation. Sometimes victims in this state are easier to handle one-on-one. If I need help, I'll get someone for sure. Thank you for your report, I'll be sure to let you know when I'm done." Trying so hard to be professional, but this man makes it so damn hard.

"Of course, Callie. You are the professional in this case, in both areas."

"Is there anything else I need to know? Has she been able to give a statement?" I ask before leaving the lounge.

Dr. Saunders returns to his screen, "The only statements the police and EMTs could get, between her rage and hysteria, is that vampires and werewolves are after her... I've never heard of such a case where both would attack the same victim."

"Alright, thank you, Dr. Saunders. I'll make sure to record my examination and see if I can calm her down to get a more formal statement and photos. Anything else?" I turn the handle on the door but wait to leave until dismissed.

"Take your time," he smiles. Such a dark smile at that. "Oh, and Callie..."

"Yes?"

"Thank you..." His tone flirty, with a touch of heat and Alpha power mixed.

Nodding my head, blushing as the heat in my center blooms more. "Happy to be of service...Galen." I say that last part quietly and walk out of the lounge quickly, missing his response, probably something inappropriate knowing him. I may not live in pack territory or be a member of the pack any longer, but I still show him the respect that he has earned and deserves.

Like I said, so glad that there is a mask mandate, I don't have a poker face, my body gives enough away as it is.

Damn that Dr. Saunders and damn my hormones.

Let's go see what I'm in for. Deep breath, time to jump into the fire...

Two

"WELL, ISN'T THIS A cluster-fuck."

Dr. Saunders really wasn't kidding about this being a bad case; they even have security posted at the door. I stand in shock at the display in front of me; the patient is in 4-point restraints and still attempting to thrash about, wide-eyed, and seems to have gone mad. Never mind the fact that she is covered in blood, various abrasions, and bite marks all over her body; she literally looks like she was mauled by an animal, or several for that matter.

"DON'T COME NEAR ME! YOU'RE ONE OF THEM! YOU'RE GOING TO HURT ME! GET ME OUT OF HERE!"

The patient is beyond reasoning. I walk into the exam room and close the door behind me.

I can do this.

Holy fuck...deep breath.

"Ma'am, I'm trying to help you. My name is Callie, I'm a nurse.

I need you to calm down so that I can clean you up and collect samples so the police can catch whoever did this to you. Are you ok with this? I need your consent before I can begin." The patient continues thrashing about as if not hearing me; if I don't do something soon, she is going to do more damage to herself than how she was brought in.

I set my gear on the counter and started to lay everything out to organize the steps for this visit. It's not that I don't like this part of my job; it's just being a nurse, a witch/empath, and part werewolf makes it very hard to deflect all of the emotions she is projecting. I can feel her fear, her rage is so strong, her anxiety, and her pain. Bile starts to rise up my throat as her emotions continue to slam into me, like an old Viking battering ram beating down the front door to a fortress.

The patient continues with her hysterics; I can't take it anymore. I walk over to the patient, place my fingertips on her forehead, and whisper a small incantation, "Et cessabit". Her nerves instantly settle and the thrashing ceases. I normally don't like to bring magic into my work, but the patient was on the verge of hurting herself, I just couldn't let her continue. Within a few seconds, the patient has calmed down enough for me to start.

She looks up at me, "Wh-what did you do to m-me?" She asks softly.

"I helped you. As I said before, my name is Callie, I'm a nurse. You are at Capital City Hospital. I also happen to be a witch; I used a little bit of magic to calm you down." I explain.

I take her hand in mind, giving it a light squeeze. "I'm also certified in working with sexual assault victims. I need to do an exam and collect samples for the police so that they can figure out who did this to you. Are you ready to begin?"

She slowly nods in agreement.

I go back to my equipment and grab the supplies needed for the first part of the exam; notepad, pen, camera, specimen containers, tweezers, and a small blue gemstone. I wrap my hand around the gemstone and invoke a truth spell so that I can be aware of the patient's honesty. I don't like using the truth spell, but since this is the Era of MeToo, all examinations and statements need to be admissible to the courts.

I hold up the stone in front of the patient, "Before we begin, there are a few things to need to inform you on. Firstly, I'm required by law to use a truth gemstone and it is required of me to let you know that I'm going to be using one today. I will also be recording this session; if there are any questions that become too difficult to answer, just say pass. Deal?"

She remains quiet and just nods. I return her nod with a small smile and place the gemstone next to her on the table. I go back to my gear and set up the camera on the tripod, angled down towards the patient.

I return to the patient with my notepad and start asking questions while examining her body. Typical demographic information: name, date of birth, home address, next of kin, place of employment, any significant other, and race. The patient remains calm during the questioning, the stone turning blue as she answers signaling her truth.

- Patient name: Kelly Baker, 22 years old. Lives in Grovestown with her parents.

- Works at the University in the library, while she takes night classes in English Literature.

- She is one out of five siblings, no significant other while in school and working.

- Race: human.

I put the notepad down, "Good job, Kelly, just a few more things, and then we are done. Now I just need you to take a deep breath, you are doing a great job. Now it's time for me to collect–"

Knock...knock...

I turn my head towards the door as I see a police uniform about to walk through. I immediately jump up from my chair and rush to the door. I'm about to send the officer away when

I finally make eye contact and realize that the officer is Forest Monroe, Capital City's very first witch crime scene investigator.

"Forest, what are you doing here?" I ask him in the doorway, not letting him pass into the room.

He and I have known each other ever since I became SANE certified a few years ago; he is one of the few officers within Capital City who assist in paranormal crimes. Him being a witch allows him to cast spells to assist in taking down the bad guys; he also happens to be a superb herb-collecting buddy, must be all that attention-to-detail crap he does at work. It's nice having someone that I can share ideas of new spells and debate earth magic versus familiar magic with, not that I can't debate with Shadow, but he tends to be biased.

Physically, Forest isn't also bad to look at either, standing about 6'1", very fit and toned; and not overly jacked like you see some of the other police officers; you can tell that he's never taken a steroid a day in his life, he's all about clean-living. Bald and clean-shaven, almost, but that's not what attracts me to him. It's his warm touch, the energy he gives off and those green-hazel eyes; those eyes practically bury right into my soul.

"I'm the one who brought her in. My partner is the one that found her in an alley way in the alley next to Dark Illusion. We believe that she have ingested some illegal contraband. I was just coming to see if you needed any help and to offer any support, or an extra set of hands," he explains with a sympathetic smile.

"As much as I appreciate the help, I honestly think the more people in this room would be a bad idea. Especially when those extra people are bigger and stronger than my patient. I don't think she would feel comfortable participating in the exam otherwise."

Deep breath.

"Look, I've got this, and I've already started. You will get my report when I'm done, just like always. Thank you for the offer, but you need to leave so I can get this done." I say exasperatedly but with a small smile.

He brings his hand up to cup the side of my face; his hand makes me feel small, and he smiles back at me.

"What ever you say princess.I'll be waiting for that report."He turns around and leaves, I quickly shut the door behind him.

Turning back to my patient, "Who was that?" She asks.

"That was Forest, he's a police officer; he and his partner found you and brought you in. He's also a good friend of mine." I explain.

She frowns, "I don't remember him."

"That's really not uncommon given everything you have been through tonight. Let's get back to this so you can get some rest." Trying to remain calm and positive. This next part of the exam is always the hardest for victims. She nods again in agreement.

The next set of questions are harder to answer, questions about what she remembers before her attack. She remembers going to work at the library on campus, coming home, changing, and meeting up with a few classmates for dinner, and then going over to Dark Illusion to celebrate the end of finals. She remembers dancing, drinking, and meeting a bunch of attractive men, but then slowly, her memory falters. She doesn't remember what they looked like or what they talked about; she remembered drinking enough that the bartender took her keys and was going to get a cab home. She was waiting for the cab outside when she heard a noise about the corner, but she didn't remember anything more.

"This is all very useful information. It's ok that you don't remember everything right now, you may never fully remember. It's best to keep a notebook with you in case something triggers your memory. The brain has a way of hiding trauma from the victim, sometimes they never fully remember."

I put my pen and notepad away and put gloves on.

"Kelly, I want you to take a few deep breaths for me. You have been through a lot; I need to collect samples and get you cleaned up. Can you hang in just a little bit longer? I'm going to start with a pelvic exam to rule out any sexual assault and injury." I release her legs from the restraints and position them into the stirrups. She takes three deep, calming breaths and I sit down on a stool at the end of the stretcher. Using my blue light flashlight, I shine the light over Kelly's pelvic area.

External examination reveals no bleeding or bruising and no semen or vaginal discharge.

Deep breath.

She wasn't sexually assaulted, relief floods through me. I collect my swabs as part of the process, though I doubt forensics will find anything alarming. "All done with the pelvic exam Kelly. You're doing great. I'm just going to collect some blood samples and swab some of those abrasions and lacerations before I get you cleaned up."

I feel like informing her of this process might be over kill, but I hate silence during this part; anything to keep her calm, the better.

"Ok. Um, nurse, I'm starting to feel a little funny. Is that normal?" She tells me as I put her ankles back in restraints. Safety first, I've been injured enough times on the job to know to get patients back in restraints as quickly as possible.

"Just hang in there Kelly, that's the magic letting you know that my spell is going to be wearing over soon. Just trying to stay calm. I'll be done as soon as I can."

I perform the specimen collection and venipuncture quickly, taking mental notes of the bruising on her arms and thighs, the width of the bite marks, and some residue of a blue powder under her fingernails. Just as I'm starting to clean up her arms, she starts fidgeting and twitching.

Damn, I need to work on a longer spell.

"TH-THEY ARE C-COMING FOR ME!!!"

She returns to shouting and thrashing. Well, I guess I'm done here, I can't cast the same spell twice. Magic can be very tricky; casting the same spell more than once has been known to have long-term adverse effects, such as inducing comas to quite the opposite of a full-blown psychotic break. I also need to conserve my energy until I can get home.

"Silentium bulla." I wave my hand at the doorway just as I finish packing up my notes and specimens. A light purple bubble forms over the doorway, acting as soundproofing so no one outside this room can hear Kelly. She is creating such a racket that I'm sure it has to be disturbing other patients and staff.

"Thank you," the security guard says to me with an appreciative smile as I pass through the bubble.

"That should last long enough for the team to give her a sedative," I reply quickly and start walking back to the nurse's station to hand in my specimens and report my findings to Officer Forest and Dr. Saunders.

Three

As I approach the nurse's station, I'm not surprised at all to find both Officer Forest and Dr. Saunders waiting for me, already discussing the case I imagine. I stand there for just a moment and they both simultaneously turn their gazes in my directions.

Handing the brown bag of specimens to Forest, "Get this to forensics. You'll have my report and recording by the end of my shift." I give him a curt nod and turn towards Dr. Saunders.

"I put a silence bubble charm on the patient's door. Once you figure out what drugs are safe to give her the spell will automatically dissipate. The spell is reactive to sound, so it will remain intact until she has calmed down."

Dr. Saunders places a hand on my right shoulder, and looks me in the eyes intensely, "Thank you, Callie. I appreciate your help with this. Based on your exam, what do you suspect?" His expression swiftly flowed from hot and steamy to cold and professional.

"I'm not a forensic expert Dr. Saunders. I can't speculate what happened," I start to give him my report, but he interrupts me.

"Callie, you're a S.A.N.E. and a witch. This isn't the first case you've ever worked on?" He says angrily.

He's going to lose control over himself, right here, right NOW!!!

His Alpha aura bursts through his control, radiating from him like a thick blanket of smog, causing me to flinch away from the two gorgeous men in front of me.

"Galen!" I choke out, reaching for Forest, and grabbing onto his arm.

The Alpha aura wouldn't normally affect witches, but where my parents are both werewolves, I got their weakness for submitting to the aura. It wouldn't be so bad if I was part of the pack, but I'm not, so it can hit me pretty hard.

Forest steps in, "Galen knock it off! Get your aura shit under control; she can't breathe man!"

As if his words hit home, Dr. Saunders instantly reels back his Alpha aura, blinking a few times completely confused as to what he had done; I take in a deep breath, it was as if an elephant was sitting on my chest. His eyes glow gold, his face goes cold as he readjusts his stethoscope around his neck.

He goes to reach out to me, but stops mid-air, "I'm sorry Callie...I didn't mean for it to get out of hand."

Forest, looking concerned, squeezes my shoulder; I nod to let him know that I am ok now.

"If you had let me finish giving you my report, I was about to tell you that I think the patient is telling the truth." I flip open my notes to a couple of pages. "She has multiple bites and gashes scattered all over her body; they should heal fairly quickly. There is some good news, she wasn't sexually assaulted. Her pelvic exam revealed no bleeding, bruising, injury, or any discharge consistent with sexual assault."

The two of them look at each other, their faces cold and flat.

Somehow, they already knew this wasn't a SANE case.

Whatever.

They start to glare at each other, like having a silent pissing contest. "Either way Forest, once you get my report this is no longer an S.A. case unless forensics reveals otherwise. I'm going to get back to my unit now and get this typed up. Forest, will I still be meeting you at the park?"

Forest looks at me with a hint of disappointment in his eyes; I've seen this look from him before, he's bailing.

"Callie, I'm sorry. I completely forgot about tonight and took on an extra shift since the full moon is so close. You know how crazy it gets." He looks at me with a smile. That smile could melt any grudge or annoyance right out of you.

"It's ok Forest, Shadow and I will be fine." I smile at him, trying to fake my emotions that I'm not a little bit disappointed about him bailing.

I turn towards Galen, who has resumed his professional composure once again, "Dr. Saunders, if you'll excuse me." Giving him a curt nod and leaving both men standing there.

***

Returning back to my workstation with my notes in hand, I look over to Brody.

"Everyone is fine. All of your patients are still alive and breathing, including that old prick in room 12. Nothing new to update." He smiles. He sees all the scribble of notes that I've taken during that exam. "Shift change is in an hour, why don't I keep your patients and let you type up your report, ok?"

"Thank you, Brody, you're the best!"

Sighs...

So much work to type up. Thankfully, Brody is the shift leader tonight for our unit, I would have felt bad if he had a normal caseload on top of mine.

"Before I forget, this came for you via messenger." Brody places a thin, long white box next to me, on top of my papers.

The box is tied together with a satin black ribbon. I hesitantly untie the ribbon and lifted the lid to reveal a single flower stem holding a small handful of black wolfsbane blossoms.

Who would have sent this to me?

Black wolfsbane is rare and expensive... I continue looking through the bad to find a business card, instantly I know who sent this. Not Dr. Saunders, who I just saw downstairs, but his other side, Alpha Galen Saunders.

Looks like I'm being summoned home, but why?

"Did the messenger say anything, Brody?"

Brody just shakes his head, ignoring my concerned look, totally engrossed with his computer. I hold up the business card to show him.

"I'm being summoned back home." I put the business card back on top of the flower and placed the lid back on the box. I can't deal with this right now; I need to get this report done. I'll deal with my summons after I manage to type all my notes up.

"Looks like no herb hunting with For-"

"Forest canceled and took on a last-minute shift because of the case that came in." I cut Brody off with a shrug. "I'll have to go home and change. I need to grab Shadow anyway; no way am I going back home without him."

Home, The Silver Crescent pack.

I don't talk about it much because of how I left. Being 18 years old at the time, and only having Shadow to watch my back, leaving was the hardest decision I ever had to make. Being a witch with werewolf-like traits made me "the black sheep" of the pack. Being the daughter of the Alpha didn't help either. I should have taken over the pack after my father stepped down, but no one would have followed me. I had been told many times that my mother had difficulties with previous failed pregnancies prior to and after my birth. It is uncommon for a werewolf pair to not have additional werewolf children, but after my birth, my mother was unable to conceive again.

So that's when my so-called friend, Galen Saunders, took over. That same night, I packed up my belongings and left with Shadow.

That was fourteen years ago. I try not to think about it, and I try like hell not to go back. My parents are given special permission during holidays and birthdays to come off pack territory to visit me. There is just no way I'm going back there without Shadow; something is up, and I need to find out what.

Thinking back to home reminds me of when I first met Shadow. And that was twenty-seven years ago...

I was five years old, walking about the forest within the pack territory. Sunlight filters through the dense foliage, giving the forest a magical feel. The peaceful sounds of birds chirping and leaves crunching underneath my feet are the only sounds to be heard. I was looking for herbs and flowers for our pack shaman, Maybelle.

She had taken me under her wing when I started exhibiting powers of being a witch, instead of that of a werewolf, like my parents and our pack. Maybelle was like me, a witch with werewolf traits, who fell in love with a werewolf. Instead of separating the two of them, the Alpha at the time allowed her to stay, so long as she became the pack shaman, healing and helping the pack when needed. That morning Maybelle sent me into the forest with my basket and a list of items that we needed to work on a spell, and to not come back until I had everything. I knew what everything looked like, but didn't know what spell needed all this.

Anytime I asked what it was for, I was always told "You will learn in time. Be patient young one."

This time my list consisted of:
- *silver maple leaves x 5*

- *sunflowers x 2*

- *wild fern x 6*

- *orange day lilies x 5*

- *black wolfsbane x 7*

Stopping in front of a huge maple tree, I rummaged through the leaves to find the first item on my list. A twig snapping on the other side of the tree causes me to freeze.

"Galen, that better not be you trying to scare me. It won't work!" I yell, placing my basket down, moving around the tree, and getting ready to fight.

A wolf with fur as dark as midnight emerges, its eyes glowing. I freeze instantly at the size of the beast, larger than any were-wolf I've ever seen. The wolf stops just a few feet from me and sniffs out in my direction.

"Hello, Mr. Wolf. Ar-Are you lost?" I stutter nervously.

"I'm not lost now, Callie." A deep masculine voice echoes in my head.

"H-how do you know my n-name?" I stumble over my words, I will not show fear to this beast, even if he could eat me in just two bites.

"I've been sent by the Goddess to find you. To be your guide, your protector, and friend now that your powers have awakened." He sits down in from of me, tail wagging and thumping forest the ground.

I take a step towards the big wolf, hand outstretched. He sniffs my hand, then gently nuzzles it with his cold wet nose.

Gross!

"If the Goddess sent you, does that mean you are to be my familiar?" Maybelle had been telling me that I would eventually meet my familiar, an animal of sorts that would help me grow and learn as a witch. I guess she was right.

He nods his head in reply.

"Would you like to help me collect herbs and flowers for a spell?"

As if answering me, he stands up, brushing up against me, his sheer size almost knocks me over. I go back and collect my basket and we start to walk along the woods.

"We are going to be great friends, Mr. Wolf, I can feel like it," I tell him as I grab hold of his fur to hold onto while walking, like holding hands with a friend.

"My name is Shadow, little one." He replies warmly in my head.

"Earth to Callie, you ok over there?" Brody's voice snapped me out of my trip down memory lane.

"Yeah, sorry. Lost in thought. Heh-heh." I look down at my papers and start focusing on typing my report.

Four

P ULLING MY JEEP INTO my driveway, I was elated to be home. Though smaller than other houses in the area, my quaint 2-bedroom house is in an unbeatable location. My daily commute consists of a leisurely 20-minute drive away from all city life, including the hospital, which allows me the perfect length of time to compartmentalize my home life from my professional.

My home, nestled amidst the natural elements, features a back deck with a view of the forest. My garden, which has gradually overtaken the front yard space for quite some time now, needs expansion to accommodate all the potions and baked goods I concoct for the club and Apothecary clients. However, upon closer inspection, it's perfect for Shadow and myself.

Walking to the kitchen, all is quiet, too quiet. Walking to the kitchen, all is quiet, too quiet.

"Shadow?"

I kick the door shut and throw my bag and gift of Wolfsbane on the counter. The house is still quiet, Shadow has not responded like he normally does.

"Shadow, I've had a really rough night. If you're trying to scare me, knock it off already." I call out through the house.

The house just remains quiet. The hair on the back of my neck rises, and my heart starts to race. I sprint to the other end of the house to our rooms. I open my bedroom door to see my room remains untouched, has always been a stark contrast to the chaos that awaits me in Shadow's room. My bed is neatly made, and my already-worn scrubs, from this week, lay in a pile on the floor. Shadow's room, however, is a scene of destruction; always has been, but this time it's far worse.

Sheets and blankets are half-shredded, tossed around like debris, and feathers fall out from their pillows. I flip the switch, casting a harsh light on the room. Shadow must have put up quite a struggle. With a roar, I slam his door shut, the vibrations pulse through the frame of our house.

A searing fury courses through my veins, igniting my magic. I need to find him.

Who could have taken him?

Whoever they are, they're in for a harsh reality check. My fingers twitch with the beginnings of a magical discharge slowly leaking out from my control. I need to call the only one who can help me find him. I make my way back to the kitchen to get my cell phone.

Me: MOM - NEED HELP! SHADOW IS MISSING!!!

Mom: Can't talk now sweetie. I've sent you a messenger, it should arrive any minute.

A messenger? What on earth is happening?

Before I can even begin to comprehend the situation, an orange orb of energy, approximately the size of an orange, materializes in the center of the kitchen. At a quick glance, the ball of energy reminds me of a fuzzy orange dust bunny with a pair of cute eyes, a creepy smile, with fangs popping out.

She sent me a will-o'-the-wisp?

This isn't a promising sign, as wisps are neither benign nor malicious, but they operate for their self-interest. They have the capacity to either assist or impede their summoner. It's akin to a coin toss when you summon one; you'll never be certain of the type of wisp you'll receive.

"I have a message for Calista Lucas-Spellcaster," it states in a low voice and settles into my outreached hand.

Grrr, she used my formal pack name.

"That's me," I tell the wisp.

"Perfect. The message is as follows: the Alpha has your Shadow. Shadow is safe and unharmed. Please do not over-react. You need to come to the pack immediately. Message complete." It reports.

"Wisp, are you able to carry a message back to the original sender? If you aren't too busy, that is."

It hovers above my hand for a minute, contemplating my request. "Yes, payment will be required in trade for service. Be snappy though," it demands.

"I can offer one drop of blood as payment. Is this accept-able?" I offer up my finger.

"Deal accepted. Message first, then payment," the wisp states.

"Please confirm who the sender was of the original message wisp. It will determine my message back to them," I inquire.

Without hesitation the wisp states, "Former Luna of the Silver Crescent pack, Maya Lucas."

"Tell her that I will be arriving within the hour and tell her thank you for the message."

I prick my finger and offer up the drop of blood as pay-ment. Witches' blood is potent and filled with various magical properties; wisps crave any power as they cannot possess it themselves. The wisp absorbs the drop of blood and vanish-es, hopefully, to deliver my message.

Since my encounter with the wisp, my anger has somewhat subsided. I find it hard to believe that Alpha Galen Saunders dared to make such a move, especially since I just received his summons today. Dr. Galen Saunders; I can't believe that he did that. I just saw him at the hospital just two hours ago and he didn't utter a word. It's one thing to summon me back to the pack formally but to invade my home, my sanctuary, and take my familiar is beyond reproach. They don't know who they're messing with.

I quickly cleanse myself with a shower and change into my armor. I can't let him get away with coming into my home and taking my familiar. I secure my hair back in a simple braid, ensuring it won't interfere with my mission. I double-check my appearance and makeup; my war paint is flawless, and my armor consists of tight dark blue jeggings, a black tank top, black knee-high boots, and as many weapons as I can fit.

I was able to fit one dagger in each boot, my 9mm in my right-side holster, and several potion bombs in my bag. I grab my silver-tipped bullwhip and staff. I think that's it, throwing my overnight bag in the passenger side of my Jeep and climbing once more behind the wheel. My body trembling from adrenaline and rage.

Deep breath...my nerves settling down.

I need to be calm before dealing with the Alpha of the Silver Crescent pack.

***

I can still hear my Dad's words as if it happened yesterday...

"It's time for this pack to have new leadership." Standing up on stage in front of the pack, my father's statement leaves us all

speechless and stunned. *"I don't say this lightly, we have a solid pack and have been this way for over two hundred years during my time as Alpha, but it's time for change."* He announces to the pack while standing up on the stage for them all to see and hear him. His voice is calm and reassuring, but I'm still surprised by his statement. Mom and I are standing behind him on the stage, along with his Beta Marcus, and his son Galen. Something just doesn't seem right, Marcus would never let this happen; but he's standing there, not doing anything.

Why is Dad stepping down?

He continues his speech about how this pack needs to experience a change in leadership to prevent our way of living from going stagnant. His next words shock me more than anything. *"It is with great pleasure to announce that I nominate my daughter, Callie to take over the pack in my stead..."*

The pack is quiet. No one utters a single word.

My Dad waves behind himself for me to step forward, I go to stand with my Dad, confusion easily readable on my face.

"She can't!"

"She is not a wolf!"

Other remarks are yelled from the pack. Yelling ensues, and fists start getting thrown up in the air. I start to panic; this pack has never accepted me as one of their own, not in the 18 years of my life. Their treatment towards me worsened after I started displaying my powers.

They are right.

I can't be the Alpha.

I'm not a wolf.

I'm a witch.

The closest to being a wolf is my familiar, Shadow.

The yelling gets louder and more intense, and anger from the pack is radiating. Marcus steps forward up behind my Dad, and whispers in his ear, *"I told you that this would never work. You can't expect them to side with you and change just overnight. Galen would be a fine Alpha." His suggestion hurts more than it should, but it's completely understandable. Galen would make a fine Alpha.*

The pack continues shouting and yelling their opinions that I'm not good enough, that I'm not worthy enough, that I'm not a wolf. I'm only 18 years old, I'm still learning to control my powers. I have never wanted to be Alpha, no matter how much my Dad forced me to train with the warriors and learn to track with the guardians. This pack will never respect me as an Alpha, I will never forgive myself if this pack goes rogue all because my Dad wants to be progressive and have me as the Alpha

I reach out through my familiar bond to Shadow...

'I think it's time we leave the pack Shadow.'

'We always knew this day would come. I'm ready when you are.' His words are just the encouragement I need; I step forward and pack to pack.

"SILENTIUM!" I shout as a purple glow erupts from my hands and blasts over the crowd, instantly the pack is silenced by my spell.

I step forward on the stage, looking forward to the pack with my chin raised. My confidence is gone, but I can feel Shadow's presence through our link.

"I will not be the next Alpha to this pack. Yes, new leadership is needed, but it will not be from me. I throw my support to the Beta's son, Galen. He would be the wisest choice for new leadership and progression for this pack." I turn and look at my Dad, giving him a quick head nod, and then walk off stage.

Galen starts to walk towards me, and with his long strides, he manages to come close to me. I hold my hand out to stop him and shake my head at him as the tears start to roll down my cheeks. This whole thing was bound to happen, might as well be today, it's only my 18th birthday after all and without a wolf, I have no place here.

The minute my last step down the stage stairs, Shadow is there for me. I climb onto his back and head to my parent'shouse to go pack up our things without a second look back to our now former pack...

My mind races with every conceivable reason Galen might have for taking Shadow, each one becoming more absurd than the last. My internal monologue grows increasingly crazier as I drive. It feels as if my hands move automatically on the steering wheel as if my mind has disengaged from the physical act of driving. As I exit the bustling cityscape of Capital City, I find myself heading into the dense, shadowy forest of pack territory. A solitary road cuts through the heart of pack territory. It was designed this way to better track any vehicles coming in and leaving.

I pull up to the entry gatehouse and wait for security to let me through.

A guard approaches my Jeep with a clipboard and radio, "Name?" He asks.

"Callie Lucas-Spellcaster. I am expected."

I leave it at that. The guard steps back from my Jeep, checking his clipboard, and radios to the main house.

After a few minutes of chatter, the guard approaches me. "All clear ma'am. The main house is..."

"I know where it is. I grew up here," I interrupt with a smile. He must be new because anyone else would have recognized the name and just let me through the gate with no explanation. He gives a nod and then returns to the gatehouse and lifts the gate, allowing me to pass.

The pack territory is laid out like a spider web, the main house located directly in the middle with the other members and families of the pack spread out into the forest. The main packhouse consists of three floors; the first floor includes the den, kitchen, dining hall, library, offices, and the mini hospital with a surgical suite, just in case. The second and third floors are bedrooms and suites for status members of the pack and the Alpha.

I pull up to the main house and park my Jeep directly in front of the door. Making it an easy get-away if I need to. I step out and take in my surroundings, noticing that nothing has changed since I left. Except that this time I seem to have a welcoming committee, my Mom and Dad. I grab my staff, leaving my bag in the Jeep, for now, I have enough weapons on me to do damage if needed, especially with my staff. I can feel myself losing my calming grip, my magic brewing as electricity sparks from my fingertips.

"Mother. Father. Where is he?!" I demand, looking them both in the eyes, letting my anger and power slip out of my control slightly.

My father stumbles slightly at the feel of my power, my mother just smiles expectingly at me.

"Your power has grown since we last saw you," she says. "You won't need your weapons. Shadow is safe and un-harmed, with our Alpha as we speak." She turns and enters the main house, expecting me to follow.

How can she remain so calm?

Before entering the house, I take notice of several pack members slowly gathering, whispering, and looking in my direction. My father adjusts himself and follows me into the house, cutting off any chance for a quick escape. Mother continues to lead us through the den, down the hallway, to the offices, mainly the Alpha's office.

She abruptly stops and turns around to face me, "You can't enter his office with weapons, Callista. It would be viewed as a challenge and we both know that you don't want that."

Another werewolf comes up to us in the hallway, bowing to my parents as a sign of respect for their previous and current status within the pack. "I can take your things to your room if you like."

He seems sincere enough. Appears to be mid-20s, muscle fit, blonde short hair, silver eyes, with tattoos on both biceps, definitely a gorgeous specimen of a werewolf, but not my cup of tea. I give him a quick once over and start handing my weapons over to my father. No way am I handing my weapons over to some were that I don't know, and like hell if I'mstaying in the main house, that's just asking for trouble.

"No offense, but I will be staying with my parents. Thank you," I say as I hand my father the last of my stashed weapons, his hands full and struggling to hold everything.

My mother places a hand on my shoulder and whispers in my ear, "Keep your staff with you and think before you act."

What wonderful advice Mother...as always, with all the sarcasm in the world.

"I think I can take it from here," I turn and tell my parents and the werewolf. The werewolf bows to my parents again and leaves. My parents don't stick around for me to knock on the door. Just as I'm about to, Galen swings open the door, startling my nerves a bit.

This version of Galen isn't the smooth and collected doctor that he is in the hospital; this version in front of me is his darker self, his Alpha self, the take-no-shit from anyone self. His Alpha aura is pulsating out of him, attempting to assert dominance over me, however my anger and my magic are matching his power and strength.

We stand there in the doorway, staring at each other, the chemistry between us is only amplified from before. Not that I'mattracted to Mr. Dark-and-Dangerous. I may be small at 5'8" compared to Galen standing in front of me, towering over me at 6'5", but with my power and anger, I feel like I can take on the world, including him.

A deep gruff voice interrupts us, "If you two are done with your pissing contest, we should probably get down to business."

Hearing that voice instantly breaks the bubble of concentration I have locked in on Galen. I push past him in the doorway, shoving the door open more, and rush up to the massive beast standing in the middle of Galen's office. Dropping my staff to the ground and wrapping my arms around his neck.

Shadow...

He's my true partner-in-crime, my best friend, the only one who has ever had my back. Shadow returns my hug by wrapping one leg around me. He's so huge that I can barely wrap both my arms around him, to compare his size would be to compare to the size of a grizzly bear.

"I'm so glad that you're ok," relief washes over me as I whisper into his ear, not letting go, afraid to let go.

"I'm fine, but we can talk, later. Alone. Alpha Galen needs to get this meeting started." He licks my cheek in reassurance. I release my death grip from Shadow and pick up my staff before returning my attention to Galen.

During my embrace with Shadow, Galen resumed his position behind his desk, littered with various documents and papers. His desk, covered with disorganized files and papers, presents a stark contrast to the organized and professional life of Dr. Saunders whom I had witnessed multiple times at the hospital.

"So? Are you going to tell me what the hell is going on or are we going to just stare at each other?" I demand an explanation, my tone dripping with sarcasm to reflect my growing frustration.

Standing here in silence, the three of us were getting awkward fast.

"Why don't you sit down?" he urges, motioning towards the vacant seat opposite him.

I falter for a brief moment, my hesitation extending longer than necessary until Galen emits a growl and Shadow nudges me towards the vacant chair. I take a seat with a disgruntled exhale. Shadow settles down beside me, ensuring that he remains in contact with my leg to offer moral support and aid in regulating my magical powers. The crucial aspect of having Shadow as my familiar is his assistance in managing my ever-expanding magic. And when my feelings are in chaos, he definitely has his work set out for him.

"So, what do we need to discuss?" I ask more politely. "Besides that you kidnapped my familiar?"

"Oh...right...Erm, look I'm sorry," Galen says nervously as he laces his fingers together, resting them on his desk. "I've already apologized to Shadow, but I need to apologize to you also. I meant no harm or disrespect by taking him the way that I did. I wasn't sure how you would react to a formal summons, and my Beta thought this approach was more direct. More direct, but the wrong course of action, obviously."

I look at Shadow, in complete shock at the apology, who gives me a single nod of approval and acceptance.

"Fine, I accept your apology."

Galen's face and posture instantly relaxed, as if he was on edge or worried that I wouldn't accept his apology and attempt to blow him up or something.

"Shadow and I briefly discussed this next subject, and it sort of goes hand-in-hand with another subject...I...I don't even know where to begin really," he stammers and stumbles over trying to get the words out. I've never seen Galen have this much trouble communicating before.

"Just get on with it!" Throwing my hands up in frustration.

Beating around the bush has never done well with me. Getting exasperated and frustrated with this whole mess. I'm just trying to play nice so that I can get out of this office already. The tension is thick, making it very stuffy and hard to breathe. With a sense of desperation, Galen turns to Shadow, his eyes begging for help, disturbed by the eerie silence in the office. It's almost like Galen is afraid the words will make the world explode. Shadow looks at me and calmly states the unthinkable.

And my world does just that, explode and crumble, and my vision turns red with rage.

Five

"MAYBELLE IS SICK. SHE's dying Callie."

WHAT?! No...this can't be happening.

I look between Shadow and Galen completely in shock and disbelief. "No. I don't believe you!" I jump out of my seat, my staff in hand and run towards the door. I need to get out of this office, I need to talk to Maybelle and confirm this with her. Tears prickle my eyes, threatening to crawl down my face.

"Callie, wait..." Galen jumps up and starts to follow me, his chair sliding backward letting me know that he is not far behind me. "There's more..."

I whip around to face him, "I don't care! I need to see her! DURATUS!" I shout as a blue pulse wave emits from my staff freezing him in his tracks.

I don't waste any time, I twist the doorknob and throw open the door. Other pack members have gathered in the hallway, showing curiosity about my visit, and eavesdropping what they could from the conversation. Not showing them any interest, I start sprinting back down the hallway to the front door and out of this house, the other werewolves move out of my way. I can smell their fear, their heightened emotions are just flowing off them like a roaring river, hitting me hard. I ignore their feelings as I rush by them, the need to get out only increasing more. I hear Shadow racing after me, his claws clicking on the hardwood floor.

I may be a witch, but my parents gave me a few of their werewolf traits besides longevity of life. Speed, strength, and the ability to heal quickly are just a few extra perks for having werewolf in my family lineage.

"Callie, wait up. There is something else we need to discuss!" Shadow calls out breathlessly, doing all he can to catch up and talk at the same time. If I didn't know any better, I would say he's gotten out of shape.

"Not now!" I yell back at him.

"It's all connected-"

I instantly halt in my tracks just as was about 500 feet away from Maybelle's house. I can see her cottage is unchanged on the outside as it was when I left. It's a small cottage located a couple of thousand feet away from the main pack house. I turn around to see Shadow, he's panting heavily. "What's all connected?"

"If you had let Alpha Galen finish his conversation, he would have told you more. The patient from this morning, that you performed SANE on, died." His tone is dark and serious.

I hate that Shadow gives Galen the title of Alpha, that werewolf doesn't deserve my respect, let alone that title right now. If he had respected me, he would have talked to me at the hospital earlier, he wouldn't have kidnapped my familiar. "She wasn't the first either, more like the third or fourth. Maybelle has been helping Alpha Galen with trying to identify the chemical found in the victim's blood that caused the victims to act combatively and recklessly." He pauses as he attempts to step closer to me, attempting to make contact.

I know what he's trying to do, he wants me to be calm.

He doesn't understand though, I need my anger. I step backward a couple steps closer to Maybelle's.

I need my anger.

I need to see Maybelle. My mind is filled with an abundance of questions that I need to ask Maybelle.

"I need to see her Shadow...alone. Go take a walk, I'll meet you are Mom and Dad's." I can feel his disappointment in my request, but I know he understands.

He nods and saunters off; I'm certain he's heading towards the woods. Hopefully to engage in his usual routine of running or hunting, which never fails to uplift his spirits.

I turn back around and walk the rest of the way to Maybelle's. *Deep breath...deep breath...one...two...three...*

Her home is nestled amidst a cluster of trees, with a vast garden enveloping tightly around her house. As I am about to knock on the front door, it swings open and reveals a sturdy older woman with flowing silver hair, eyes the color of a stormy sky, and a complexion warmed by the sun's embrace over the years.

I sense a noticeable absence of energy within her' when I extend my own magical powers toward her, there is no reciprocation or connection. Her staff in hand is used more as a walking stick or cane these days, unable to hold any magic.

She smiles up at me, "Good evening Callie. I've been expecting you," she says softly stepping out of the doorway, allowing me to come in and follow her.

Her house hasn't changed on the inside either, with minimal furniture, flowers and herbs hanging upside down, drying out for future use in potions and spells, and candles burning everywhere giving off a soft magical glow. She waves a hand to the kitchen table and chairs, pouring tea into mugs for us.

Sighing as I take a seat feels just like old times. The last time I was here was to tell her that I was leaving the pack, with Shadow and heading into the city. And that conversation did not go well.

She sets my mug in front of me and takes a seat across the table as if nothing is wrong. "Shadow said that you're dying," surveying her up and down, "I don't understand, you look great, but I don't feel any magic in you anymore. It's like you aren't a witch anymore; you have no aura anymore. How is that possible?"

"Well, he's right to an extent. I am dying, my magic is gone." She explains fatherly bluntly. "The magic that keeps us witches living longer than human lives is gone, so now I am aging as a human and will one day move on to the Afterlife. Before losing my magic, I was helping Alpha Galen figure out what drug people are coming into contact with within the city that is causing them to die several hours later. All I've been able to come up with is that it's a natural blue herb crushed into a powder and then mixed with something synthetic. I think that's why my magic is gone. I think the drug affects supernaturals differently than humans. But I can no longer help as I don't have my magic anymore."

"I don't understand how you lost your magic in helping Galen. Can't you just get it back?!" So many more questions are bubbling just under the surface, yet I feel like the rug has been pulled out from under me, forcing me into a corner that I can't get out of. My mind reels, spinning more questions:

Who is behind all this?

Why would someone do this?

What is the end game to all of this?

Maybelle sips her tea, looking as calm as ever. "No Callie, I can't get my magic back. I'm not exactly sure how I lost it in the first place. I don't know if I lost it from trying to help Alpha Galen, or if the Goddess has decided that it's my time. All I know is that I don't have long, that's why I asked Alpha Galen to send for you."

This isn't making any sense, Maybelle is a vessel of all things pure and good, I can't imagine why the Goddess would do this to her, especially amid a drug crisis.

"I still don't understand why you think you can't get your magic back…" I take a sip of my tea; something just doesn't seem right. How can she be so calm? And the house is too quiet. Wait… "Maybelle, where's Raven?" Raven is to Maybelle what Shadow is to me; a familiar, a friend, a part of my soul.

Maybelle takes another sip of her tea before responding, "She is gone. The Goddess called her to the Afterlife about a week ago. The same night that I lost my magic; that's how I know I'm not getting my magic back. You and I both know that it's dangerous for a witch to channel magic without a familiar. I've never been able, unlike you when you were younger."

I stare at her in surprise; I can't believe she remembered that I started exhibiting magical abilities before meeting Shadow. I am sad for Maybelle, her acceptance of the death of her familiar and of her never practicing magic again is just too hard for me to accept. I reach across the table and take her hand in mine, she's ice cold despite drinking her tea.

"I'm so sorry Maybelle, about everything. Why didn't you call me or send a wisp?"

"You know there is no cell service here, why does there need to be when all you need is within pack territory? Besides no magic means I couldn't send you a wisp. Alpha Galen and I don't want the pack to know just yet. I can still contribute to the pack but making herbs, tonics, and salves." She says with more positivity than I would have been able to muster. "Honestly Callie, I'm ready. I've outlived many pack members and more lovers than I care to share. But none of that matters now, you're here now. I just wish Alpha had used more sense and tact to get you here." She chuckles.

We sit there for several minutes, enjoying the quiet, our tea, and each other's company. She looks up at me, "Well I guess we should get down to business and discuss what's to happen next."

"What do you mean?"

"Well, I'm dying child, I need to train the next Shaman for the pack-" She starts to explain.

Lightbulb... That's why I'm here.

"WOAH! No way! I can't be the next Shaman. I left the pack, well more like delicately pushed out of THIS pack!" I interrupt her. She silences me by raising her hand to me.

"Alpha Galen and I have discussed that you should return as the pack Shaman, if you wanted and with proper training of course. However, it is your decision, but it would be nice to have you back. You already know so much more than any other witch I know who carries a quarter of your power and potential." She starts yammering as if my world hasn't exploded enough already today; my mind and body have just gone into shock. I'm not hearing anything that she is saying.

"Maybelle, I'm flattered. Truly. But I have two jobs, at the hospital and my online Shopify orders. I've made a life outside this pack. Shadow and I moved on-"

"You still have friends and loved ones here child. Just as you did before." She interjects.

Deep breath.

She isn't going to just let this go.

"I need to think this over and discuss ALL of this with Shadow. I need some air," excusing myself from the table and heading towards the door, "how much time do you believe you have before the Goddess will call for you to the After-life?"

She looks up at me, smiles, and shrugs, "One never knows dear. I feel colder and colder every day and myself getting slower."

Leaving her house with more questions than answers, I welcome the fresh air as I step out into the night. Darkness has fallen, how did I lose track of time? As my eyes start adjusting to the darkness, I make my way back towards the direction of my parents, which is on the other side of the pack house. I should go see Alpha Galen; he owes me answers.

A lot of answers.

A twig snaps in the distance as a pair of golden eyes appear from around a tree, I stop in my tracks, frozen in fear of the beast that is right ahead of me.

Friend or foe?

I use my magic to summon a golden ball of energy to throw in defense if needed. I've had a crappy day and I refuse to be pushed around by anyone with a grudge now. I call out to the beast, "I see you over there. Come out, slowly."

The golden eyes move cautiously from behind the tree to reveal a massive gray Timberwolf with minimal red marking s.The markings are not traditional for this pack, most of the werewolves here have a lot more red, which means that this beast is Galen...

"Shift," I demand the wolf.

A growl erupts from the wolf, low and deep. Slowly the fur recedes, bones snapping back, paws turning into hands and feet, skin glowing, reflecting off my energy ball. Once transformed, the crouched-over being in front of me stands to reveal Galen.

Absolutely naked...

Gulp...

And here I thought that he was gorgeous at work, in scrubs and that white doctor coat of his; boy, was I wrong! Galen looks even more deadly than he did in his office. With the moonlight peeping through the trees, I can make out all of his ripped muscles including his six-pack, and further south, his erection.

I gulp again and flush with embarrassment taking notice of the size of his erection. I can't remember when I last saw such a man naked outside of work.

"Are you done gawking? We need to talk," he demands.

Sure thing, you bet we need to talk...

I just nod and wave my arm out in the direction of the pack house, signaling to him that he should lead the way.

He quickly shifts back to his wolf form and takes off running to the pack house. I close my fist around the energy ball, absorbing back the power used to create it. I slowly start making my way to the pack house.

I need to have a conversation with Galen before I can sleep tonight. I just hope that once we do have this conversation that I WILL be able to sleep.

Alone with him in his office could be dangerous...

Six

I T WAS CLOSE TO 3 AM before I finally flopped down into my own bed at my parent's house. I've been up for almost 24 hours now, seeing how I came here right after work yesterday. I can't stop thinking about my discussion with Maybelle and Galen. I look over to the smaller bed in my room, Shadow appears to be asleep.

The image of Galen, or should I say Alpha Galen, standing naked in front of me is permanently etched in my mind. Goosebumps and heat arise deep within me, excitement flows throughout my body.

Sighs.

He is the last person that I should be thinking about...

'If you keep thinking about whatever or whoever you are thinking about, your heart is going to beat right out of your chest,' Shadow states as he lifts his head in my direction. *'So how did your meeting go?'*

"You mean meetings, plural. I met up with Galen after talking with Maybelle. It's easier to show you. Come here." I roll over to allow Shadow up in my bed. The bed sinks and creaks under his weight as he climbs in. I rest my hand on his head.

"Ostende occurens cum Maybelle," I whisper as my mind fills with flashes of memory, from my perspective, of our meeting giving Shadow the ability to see through my eyes.

He whimpers as he watches the memory flash through my mind again, I know how attached he has gotten to Maybelle and Raven. I had always teased him about how he and Raven could have been mates in another life.

After the memory fades, the connection of the spell snaps like a rubber band. A single tear runs down his muzzle. I scratch behind his ear some and pet his head for comfort. "I'm so sorry Shadow. I know how much Raven meant to you."

A low whine escapes from him, eyes closed. *'Yes, well we aren't meant to live past our charges. And your meeting with Alpha Galen went well I assume. I can smell him on you, he must have gotten close.'*

I flush again with embarrassment, resting my hand back on his head, "Ostende occurens cum Galen." The flashes of memory invade my mind again, Shadow simply watches...

Galen sits behind his desk, in full Alpha mode and fully dressed now.

Well isn't that a pity... his eyes appear darker than earlier today, like he hasn't told me all that there is to know.

"I..."

"I..."

We both start to say at the same time and chuckle. I smile at him meeting his eyes. He waves his hand at me, allowing me to go first. How very generous of you and uncharacteristic, what are you up to Galen?

"Sorry I didn't let you finish earlier in our first meeting" I start to say, "but when Shadow said that Maybelle is dying, I just had to go see her..."

"It's ok, really," He interrupts me. "I should have expected such, it's part of why I let Shadow tell you." He adjusts in his chair uncomfortably, "But there is more we need to discuss."

"Ahh yes, Maybelle told me that she has been helping you, but she lost her magic and is now dying. I'm assuming that's why you asked me here?" I meet his gaze, waiting patiently for him to dig himself out of this shit hole of a mess.

"I meant to talk to you at this hospital, but I didn't know how. I'm the Alpha; I'm not very good at asking for help, and you can be quite intimidating. I should have listened to your mother, she said that you wouldn't refuse a formal summons..." he states nervously.

"When talking to my Beta, he felt a more direct approach would be necessary and took Shadow. For which I'm sorry, again." He continues to ramble on more, but I'm distracted by the fact that this strong, confident man finds me intimidating if the man only knew what he does to me.

I still find it hard to believe that Galen couldn't talk to me, he's never had trouble being professional at the hospital, except for today, that is.

He gets up from his chair, walks around his desk, and leans against the front of his desk, his legs and feet in a large stance, just a few inches away from me. His form just towers over me, such a dominating stance to take. A heat starts to kindle, deep in my core.

"What do you want from me?" Dying to get to the point so that I can get out of this office and far away from him, except my parent's house is next door and not far away enough.

He crosses his arms over his chest, his muscles bulging beneath his shirt. "With Maybelle unable to perform any magic and dying, the pack will need a new Shaman..."

"No! Galen, I can't!" I interrupt him, his only response is to growl. "I left this pack for a reason; they won't listen to me let alone let me help them. I made a new life for myself. I have friends."

Another growl escapes from him, "If you would let me finish for once Callie," he takes a deep breath. "I'm not asking you to come back, Maybelle's son, Ajax is going to take over as pack Shaman. However, he's very new to the magical and healing arts, he has a lot to learn, but I'm confident in his potential."

"Well, it sounds like you don't need me then," I say and start to rise out of the chair.

He instantly leans forward, placing both hands on each side of the arms of the chair, "I'm not done..."

Holy crap, he's too close. I can smell his earthy musk, my core ignites, I need out of this room...NOW!

"The SA victim that was brought into the hospital today, the one that you tended to, died. I'm sorry Callie. We couldn't figure out what chemical was in her system in time. She thrashed around so hard in her restraints that she managed to snap her neck, killing herself instantly. There was nothing that we could have done." He sympathizes. "She was the third victim this week."

"I-I didn't know. I wasn't assigned to anyone else but her this week. So you want me to help you how?" I'm so confused.

"Grrr. I-I need your help with Ajax. He needs help with training to be the next Shaman. And I need help at the hospital in case another victim comes in. I need you to keep them calm, spelled if you must, until we can figure out what it is thatwe're dealing with." His demeanor was calm but very close to being shattered by frustration, and his eyes pleading me to help me. I don't know if he has noticed that I'm still trapped under him in this chair.

The heat building between us, chemistry forming, clouding my judgment, "If I agree to do this, what do you expect of me? I'm not saying yes or no, but I need to consider my options and discuss this with Shadow." I need to do this carefully and consider what I might have to give up if we have to return to the pack.

"Well as I've stated before, Ajax needs more training in potions, healing tonics, and spell-casting. The problem is that Ajax doesn't have a familiar, so that's his first step right there." He adds.

"Wait...you want Ajax to be the pack Shaman and receive training, but he doesn't have a familiar? How old is he? If he had any magical potential, he would have started exhibiting powers and the Goddess would have sent him a familiar. That's how it works. You can attempt to summon one, but typically the Goddess sends one to you once you start showing your powers." I explain.

Galen steps back and leans against his desk. His face is furrowed with confusion and disappointment. Maybe Galen didn't know all this about witches? Maybe Ajax doesn't have the potential like he thinks. "But you were exhibiting your powers way before Shadow came along."

"I'm different, it's about bloodlines and old magic. I don't feel like getting into all the details. What I can tell you is that Shadow has helped me grow immensely as a witch. There are many spells and potions that I wouldn't do if he wasn't around to help me channel the amount of power needed for them.

"This is a lot to ask, if Ajax does hypothetically have potential, you're asking me to train him like Maybelle trained me, which took 13 years before I was on my own. And I'm still learning, there are hundreds of spells that Maybelle does, well used to do that I've never even attempted before".

I get up from my seat and turn my back on Galen, heading towards the door. He reaches and grabs my left arm firmly. His touch sends goosebumps over my skin and butterflies in my stomach. I can feel my heat deep inside react, burn, to his touch. Don't do it...

Galen takes a step towards me, pressing himself up against my backside. He leans forward and whispers in my ear "Just *think about it, this pack needs your help...I need your help." He sniffs my hair and loosens his grip on my arm, but not completely letting go. "You smell so good; I had almost forgotten." His words whisper into my ear and slither to my core, causing my body to ache like it hasn't in a long time; back when we were teenagers, he had no clue about the feelings I had for him back then. We had no clue as to what we were doing.*

He slowly starts to caress small circles on my right side with his other hand. He's trying to distract me and playing on my emotions to get me to say yes.

I know he doesn't mean any of this, he's had so many chances to talk to me. I need out of this office, but he makes me feel different... He starts to nuzzle at my neck, rubbing his chin along the side of my neck slowly with his barely visible five o'clock shadow.

"Galen...don't start something that you can't finish. I need time to think. It's the least you can do."

He nods his head against my neck, kisses my neck with a small bite at the end that almost pushes me over the edge, and then he lets go of my arm and allows me to walk out of the office...

Silence fills the room as I process the memory again and allow Shadow time to draw his own conclusions.

'So, Galen still has feelings for you,' Shadow blurts out after a few minutes.

"Is that all you took from that? Really? What are your thoughts besides that?" I throw back at him.

'Mmm...just sounds like an excuse to get you back to the pack or to get into your pants. However, I am worried about the slew of victims piling up.' He pauses and just rests his head on my bed. Shadow has been doing that a lot lately, resting, maybe he's getting old. *'Let's just sleep and discuss this in the morning with Maybelle. Maybe she can enlighten us with more about Ajax?'*

He suggests as he climbs down from my bed and goes back to his.

I'm surprised by his response but can't say that I disagree either. I'm worried though, normally Shadow is more willing to let his opinion be known. This behavior seems off like he's hiding something. Or maybe he is just upset by the news of Raven. I'll need to keep an eye on him and press the issue if his behavior starts to interfere with his decision-making ability.

I lay my head against my pillow and start to do my nightly meditation body scan. It doesn't last more than a few minutes as I welcome the darkness of sleep.

Seven

"YOU GOT IN LATE last night, I'm surprised to see you up this early," my Dad says over his cup of coffee and newspaper as I come down the hallway, into the kitchen for breakfast with Shadow right on my heels.

"Morning Dad," I grumble walking towards the door to let Shadow out to do his business. I look at the living room clock, 8 AM. UGH... I flop down into a chair at the kitchen table next to Dad. He hands me part of the paper without even looking away from what he's reading. Mom comes over and brings me a cup of lemon tea and a plate of eggs and bacon.

"Thanks, Mom." She smiles at me before taking a seat across the table from me.

"Isn't this nice, having the whole family together? It's been so long." She smiles and takes a sip of her tea. "So...how did last night go?" She is so nosy, always has been. I just roll my eyes and dig into my breakfast. Can't keep any secrets in this house, or this pack for that matter.

Looking at my parents, it's as if time has frozen. They both look amazing, Dad must be keeping up with training because he is still fit as ever, just barely getting flicks of gray in his hair and beard. And Mom just looks astonishing. She is still fit and toned, all while still maintaining some curves; at least I know where I get my curves from. They are that adorable older couple cliche. They found each other later in life, they are both second mates to each other. Both of their first mates have been called to the afterlife, I never truly asked how and never really cared to ask, it was just something not discussed in this house. Mom and Dad didn't have any children before they met each other and even then waited over a century before having me. I guess being a werewolf gives you that opportunity to wait to have children with the right person. One day I hope to be as lucky as them.

"Things went as well as expected. I'm still in shock and still processing it all," I reply as I drink my tea. "Why didn't you guys tell me about Maybelle?"

Dad looks over at Mom. No one says anything for a minute, you can see them having a mind-link conversation, probably trying to cover their own asses. Finally, Dad says "Maybelle and Alpha Galen told us not to say anything until they had a plan. If you ask me, their plan was stupid."

"Hush dear...Mind your tongue" Mom interrupts over Dad.

"Since when do either of you listen to anyone? You used to be the Alpha and Luna of this pack, you never take orders from anyone!" I'm baffled that we are even having this conversation.

"Things have changed since you left dear," Mom says with a smile, trying to remain her usual positive and upbeat self, but I can see right through it.

"No kidding things have changed..."Dad grumbles into his coffee. We sit there in silence for a few moments, Mom and Dad reading the paper and drinking their coffee while I eat. I see them exchange glances now and then as if I don't know that they are talking.

"So, what can you tell me about Ajax? Alpha Galen wants me to train him to be the next pack, Shaman." I break the silence with this statement. The look exchange between them is interesting. Shock? Confusion? Both?

"Erm...that's going to be hard to do, seeing how Ajax is a shifter and Alpha Galen's third in command. He's one of our finest warriors, I've never seen him show any signs of potential for the gift that you possess. He's due to participate this morning in our training exercises if you want to come see for yourself." Dad suggests.

I immediately jump up from the table, making my way toward the door, and my powers and anger come roaring back to life. And here I thought I was going to have a good morning with my parents and see some of my old friends. Fat chance of that now... I don't know what Alpha Galen is playing at, but he knows that you can't be a shifter and a witch.

There has never been such a thing before, you're either a shifter, a witch, or a human. The only reason even I possess werewolf traits is because of my parents both being werewolves and the only reason that I'm not a shifter is because our lineage dates so far back that once every couple of centuries a witch is reborn in the family. The only magic shifters have ever been able to possess is the ability to shift into their wolves, speed, strength, and longevity of life.

I pull a small twig out of my pocket and give it a shake, transforming it into my full-sized staff. I slam the staff end down to the floor, magically changing my clothes from pajamas to tight jeans, a black tee shirt, and black ankle boots. "Honey, just take a deep breath. You need to keep a leveled head about all this. You know what happens when you lose control..." Mom shouts to me, but it's too late, I'm already out the door heading to the pack house to take on Alpha Galen.

Shadow reappears at my side within a few steps out the door and jumps in front of me to stop me. *'What's wrong now?'*

"Did you know that Ajax is a shifter?" I ask him as I walk around his giant form.

'If he is a shifter then why did Alpha Galen want him to train as the next Shaman? It's not possible and I would know, I've been around for a while.'

"Why don't we just go ask him ourselves?" I say with as much snark and anger as I can possibly muster this early in the morning.

'You need to relax and take a deep breath. No need to go in there all hot and heavy and do something stupid.' He brushes up against me, scooping my hand to rest on his head, taking some of my anger. This is why witches need familiars, they help keep us calm and in control. They also have the ability to utilize the small amount of energy drawn off their witch and can morph it into magic for themselves.

Shadow has been a familiar for a long time, he has told me many times that I'm his third witch. When I ask him what happened to his other charges, he just tells me that the Goddess has called them to the afterlife. From what I've learned in my training, familiars can outlive their witches, but it is extremely rare for a witch to outlive their familiar, something about the bonds formed with their familiars and their ability to perform magic. Maybelle is a perfect example; she lost her magic and familiar within the same night and now she is dying a slow human death.

'Feel better?' He knows I do. I nod, taking a moment to do some deep breathing exercises to recenter myself. *'Now if you'll excuse me, I'm going to take a run. I don't know what has gotten into you lately, but you need to get a grip. I can't keep taking your anger away without a price.'* He ends the mind link and trots off into the woods.

I can tell he's mad, as he has the right to be. I don't know what has gotten into me lately, maybe it's the full moon cycle coming up or something. I've been on edge a lot, I've been having to use magic more. With my staff in hand, I continue on my way to the pack house, but this time with a calmer head and at a slower pace. I need time to think about what I'm going to say and not just fly off the handle like I normally do.

Within just a few feet of the pack house, I see a small group of people gathered around, sitting on the ground. Maybelle is in the middle of the group, standing, and talking to the group. Curious about what is going on, I walk over to the group, only to find that it's a meditation group. Everyone is sitting comfortably on the ground, eyes closed and arms resting in their laps. Maybelle occasionally walks around the group guiding the group through a focused body scan. I start to walk away when Maybelle waves a hand over for me to join. I nod and sit on the outskirts of the group, not wanting to draw attention to myself.

Maybelle's voice is very calm, hypnotizing, and relaxing. Listening to her in the guided exercise reminds me of Yoda teaching young padawan learners to reach out to the force. The session ends after a few minutes, and the shifters dissipate slowly, thanking Maybelle for the session and leaving me standing there alone.

"Callie dear, is there something I can help you with?" She asks with a smile, holding herself up with her staff.

"Ajax is your son and a shifter, right? Why does Galen think that Ajax can train to be the next pack Shaman? Or is there something that I'm missing?" I bombard her with questions as calmly as I can.

"Why don't we go take a walk and discuss this with Alpha Galen? You know, behind closed doors, where wolf ears can't hear us?" She replies with a smile and starts to walk toward the pack house.

I follow behind her, keeping quiet, waiting to ask my questions. Maybelle seems slower today, I just saw her yesterday and already I notice a difference in her. Besides walking more slowly and cautiously, she seems to have more gray in her hair and her skin has paled more. I'm worried about her, at this rate she doesn't have long, maybe a week or two.

'*Shadow?*' I reach out with my mind to find him.

'Everything ok?' He responds quickly.

'Maybelle looks and seems worse today. I'm about to meet with her and Galen. Can you go find Ajax and keep an eye on him? I want to know what kind of shifter/person we are dealing with. He wouldn't just volunteer for this type of training, no one would. I'm worried that something else is going on. I don't want any surprises.' I explain.

'Sure thing, sounds like a good idea. He shouldn't be too hard to miss at this morning's warrior training.' He closes the mind-link. I can tell that he was eager for something to do, it's why he and I make such a great team.

Maybelle and I continue our walk in silence, enjoying the sunshine and each other's company. Honestly, I can't remember the last time that Shadow and I took time out from life and work to just enjoy the fresh air in the forest. It seems to have been ages, but not here on pack territory, time seems to have stopped. It feels good to be back here, even if none of my former friends have approached me. Not like I've given them any opportunity to either.

After what seems like ages, we arrive at the far side of the arena, about a few hundred feet from the pack house. There is a group of the pack gathered around; Warrior training, I remember it well. The group of shifters are gathered around in a circle, paired off to spar against each other. I notice Dad in the center giving instructions, just like he used to. But that's not what catches my attention, Galen is there with his warriors. Heat and goosebumps rush over my skin in memory of last night's encounter.

As we step closer to the group, I notice Shadow in the middle of the circle, the fighters have stopped to observe. Shadow is paired up with a shifter I don't recognize. He's a very tall, with dark hair, dark eyes, and very ripped muscular shifter, standing in just shorts with sweat already rolling down his body, including his glorious six-pack. Hot damn... *'Shadow, what are you doing?'* I mind-link in a panic.

'You said to find out what kind of shifter Ajax is. Well, say hello to Ajax.' He retorts giving the shifter a head nod, never losing eye contact with his opponent. The shifter in front of Shadow is already breathing heavily, whereas Shadow barely looks phased by the exercise.

'That's Maybelle's son? Need any assistance, don't want you losing to a shifter and giving us a bad name.' I chuckle to him.

'That won't be necessary. I've already watched him against some of the others, he tends to leave his left side open. And his speed isn't much against mine. I might have to dial it down a little just to think he might have a chance.' He laughs back before closing our link.

"Oh, look at that, Ajax and Shadow are sparring. This should be interesting to watch." Maybelle says to me as she walks towards the group, who instantly part ways for her. The respect these shifters show to Maybelle is amazing, it's going to be hard for the pack to accept anyone as the next Shaman. I stay close to Maybelle, feeling everyone's eyes on me as the session starts.

Dad gives Ajax a head nod. Ajax starts to shift. He churches down on his hands and knees. His bones start snapping, popping, and elongating. His skin starts to stretch and give way to his beautiful red-gray fur coat. I've never seen a shift happen in slow motion before unless he's trying to show off. Once Ajax is fully shifted, a red-gray Timberwolf stands almost the size of Shadow. One would definitely argue that he is as big as Galen in wolf form. A low growl rumbles out of Ajax.

'You sure you can handle him, buddy? I'd hate to lose my familiar.' I link to Shadow out of caution.

'Just be ready to heal him. This will go fast.' He replies and chuckles more. I close the link allowing him to concentrate.

And it did go fast, just as Shadow had predicted.

The two wolves start by circling each other. The shifters watching start whispering, and I hear bets being placed. None of these wolves have ever seen what Shadow can do, and they are all betting against him. I know that Ajax hears what's going on in the group, and a wave of over-confidence and ego boost rolls off him, hitting me square in the chest; all men are the same, no matter the species. I shrug it off and roll my eyes; this shifter is going to be sore later.

Ajax lunges quickly for Shadow, who turns and kicks with his hind legs just as Ajax's front legs would have made an impact. Shadow's kick lands solidly against Ajax's left side, sending Ajax skittering away but not defeated. Ajax shakes himself, a small dirt cloud coming off from where he had landed. Ajax doesn't wait to recover, he kicks off the ground and leaps through the air, landing back in front of Shadow. He's breathing heavily, snarling and growling as if to intimidate Shadow. He attacks again with full force headfirst in a flurry of teeth snapping at Shadow. Shadow moves twice as fast around him and before Ajax knows what is going on, Shadow grabs his left hind quarter, sinking his teeth in deep, and whips him around, letting him go and fall with a loud thud across from the group.

Blood drips from the wound on his leg. In wolf form, Ajax attempts to stand but is unable to bear weight on his injured leg. "Shadow is the winner!" Dad announces with a smile, "Ajax shift back." He shifts back to human much faster this time completely naked, the injury must be excruciating. Ajax instinctively reaches for his leg attempting to stop the bleeding, growling from the pain, but not crying as I would have expected. Either he has a high pain tolerance or he's putting on a brave face, either way, call me not impressed...

Rolling my eyes, "MOVE ASIDE!" I yell as I push through the shifter to kneel next to Ajax. "You're an idiot." I take his hands off the wound and replace it with mine. Solid teeth marks have gashed his outer thigh, if Shadow had gripped the inner part of the thigh, he would have nicked his femoral artery and bled out. I close my eyes and concentrate, allowing my magic to fill me up, and I whisper, "Sana..." My hands glow a pale green as his wound starts to heal.

There is no vibration of potential magic felt as I heal him, just as I experienced with Maybelle. Ajax has no potential to learn magic or be the pack Shaman. His wound heals within a few minutes, my hands stop glowing as I dissipate the energy needed.

I stand up, towering over Ajax lying on the ground, "You never stood a chance against him you know. He's over 200 years old. He's assisted his witches in wars before you and I were even born. You're lucky though, he was holding back...A lot." Shadow was right, the fight was quick. As I turn to walk away, I lock eyes with my Dad and Galen, head-bow out of respect to them both, and continue to the pack house. Galen can catch up with me this time.

Eight

"**H**E CAN'T BE THE pack Shaman."

I blurt out breaking the silence. Sitting in Galen's office with Maybelle is just as tense and uncomfortable as it was yesterday. Galen sitting behind his desk and Maybelle in the chair to my left, both looking at me to explain myself. "When I was healing him just now, I felt no vibration, no potential of magic except that of what makes him a shifter."

Galen just continues to sit there, pondering what I've just declared. I would say I'm sorry to burst your bubble, but I'm not Mr. Hotstuff... Galen turns his attention to Maybelle, "Did you know this?"

"I suspected as much, but I had no way of knowing for sure." She waves her hands up in surrender, "No magic, remember?" She chuckles and smiles over to me. "Callie, will you be the pack Shaman? Or at least for the interim?"

They both look at me. I would say that I'm shocked, but I'm not. I feel like this was planned out by them already, I'm just more irritated and annoyed for them wasting my time. It's so hard to say no to Maybelle and she knows this, but the pack will never accept me back. At least not the whole pack collectively. My only connection to this pack is my parents, Maybelle, and Galen. At least I think Galen is on my side, hard to tell these days. The rest of the pack would never accept me as their pack Shaman or put their trust in me after how I left.

"I..."

"Wait..." Galen interrupts me, "Let me make you a proposition. You continue to work at the hospital in the city, helping me take care of any victims that come in through the ER, helping me solve these murders as much as you can, all while supplying the pack with potions and salves or whatever you can in your spare time for the pack. You can continue to live in a cottage off-pack territory. All until we find your replacement."

"What do I get out of all this? It's not like I have a lot of extra free time to begin with, I do have a second job and a life outside of my work at this hospital. There are other shifters and businesses within the city that rely on my second job." I explain.

"What do you want Callie?" He asks coldly.

"I want access to the forest, there are herbs and plants in there that I'm not able to grow in my garden at home." I counter without any hesitation. The forest is magical all by itself, it's the same forest where I met Shadow. The wisps live in the forest, as well as other magical beings, ones that don't feel safe anywhere else. Having access to plant life would greatly improve my spells and energy levels for me.

Galens sits there staring at me. "Granted." He states after a few breaths, "But only if you accept the role as pack Shaman, even if it is only for the interim."

Witches who aren't born into a pack aren't typically easy to find, let alone train to be a pack Shaman. It takes years of training, and it is typically started before the previous Shaman dies or loses their magic so that they can pass on their knowledge. Much like a Jedi master showing and teaching the ways of the force to a Padawan apprentice.

Galen stands up with me, moves around his desk, and grabs my hand, slipping a piece of paper into my palm. "Thank you, Calista," he whispers into my ear before kissing my cheek and allowing me to leave. I blush from the heat of that small and simple kiss. He continues to be a gentleman and opens the door for me, I nod my head out of respect and leave his office, shoving the note he slipped to me into my pocket.I don't stop walking until after I'm several paces away out the main door. The other shifters eye me as I leave, and fresh air hits me. I didn't realize how warm that office was until I stepped outside. Shadow rejoins me and we make our way into the woods, heading towards the lake deep within the forest.

'Are you ok?' Shadow links to me.

Sighs...

'Yeah, I think so. I just don't know what to do. I want to help the pack and help Galen and Forest solve these murders, but I'm only one witch. And I have other responsibilities as well.' Shadow doesn't respond to me; he knows that I'm just venting and needing time to think everything out. We continue to walk in silence to the lake.

The lake comes into view, formed in the shape of a crescent. That's how this pack got its name, the lake is shaped like a crescent moon, and no one knows if it was man-made, or if it is one of the mysteries of nature. I sit on the grassy bank, listening to the birds and forest, Shadow joins right next to me. I remember the crumpled piece of paper that Galen slipped to me.

Meet me at the lake tonight.
Like we used to.
-Galen

'Seems pretty obvious to me what Alpha Galen wants,' Shadow snorts.

'He just wants me here to be the pack Shaman. That's it, all for the good of the pack. No matter our years of friendship and history.' Stuffing the note into my pocket.

'So, when are we heading home? There are people in the city that need your potions and powders for the upcoming full moon, not to mention your brownies.' He adds.

'I know, I know Shadow. I told Galen and Maybelle such already. That's why I asked for time to think about all this, I already have so much on my plate.'

Sighs...

'Let's go collect some herbs, we're leaving in the morning.' I stand up and start making my way back into the forest.

Shadow is right, there are plenty of shifters in the city that are counting on me. But there is still this feeling deep down that I just can't ignore. Like when Galen asked me for help, I knew that it was for the pack, but there was a burning deep down that made me think that there was more to it.

Maybe it is more obvious than I realize, maybe Galen does want more than for me to be the pack Shaman. Or maybe he is just being a dick and pulling on my heartstrings? It's hard to get over a guy who has only ever viewed you as a friend and took over your pack when they wouldn't accept a witch as their leader. Some things never change...and the same goes for people.

***

By the time Shadow and I get back to my parents, it's time for dinner, which Mom has already made up and kept warm in the oven. Dinner with my parents is done in silence, I know that they are just having a private conversation about me or whatever. Shadow ditched dinner to go hunt with some shifters he met today, it's so uncanny how they will accept him as my familiar, but not me as a witch with werewolf parents.

Ugh, whatever.

I'm just glad that at this moment that my parents aren't pushing me to talk, because honestly, I don't know what to say to them after the day that I've had.

Dinner goes by quickly; I clear the table and do the dishes for my Mom. "Honey, we are going for a run with some of the other older couples in the pack," she calls out to me from the door. "Leave the door unlocked if you go out or get back in before we do."

"Ok Mom, have fun. I'm actually going to grab a shower before I head out for a little bit-"

The front door makes a small click as it shuts behind my parents leaving.

Ok, nice talking to you too...

And with that, the house is all to myself.

The hot shower feels so good, like washing away all my problems and taking them down the drain. If I could only stay in this shower forever. I'm conflicted about how I feel about meeting Galen at the lake tonight. What is so important and secretive that we have to meet at our old hang-out spot? Washing my hair in lavender shampoo my thoughts drift back to last night in Galen's office, him nuzzling my neck, his hand on my body, I flush with heat once more deep inside my core. It's been over fourteen years since I left the pack, that man has no right to have this effect on my body.

Getting out of the shower, I wrap my towel and make a dash to my room to see, "SHADOW!!! That's so gross!" I shout as I walk in on my familiar cleaning himself. This is not the image I want burned into my brain, this is why we have separate rooms at our house. I know he's a wolf, but it's still gross that he has to lick himself, and on my bed too. "Get out! I have to get dressed." I point towards the door and slam it shut after he runs out.

UGH, familiars!

Turning back towards my bed there is a red sundress with white flowers laid out on my bed already. Mom must have laid it out for me knowing that I might be seeing a certain someone tonight. Like I said there are no secrets in this pack. I wouldn't be surprised if no one was at the lake tonight, except us.

Us.

Alone with Galen.

He will probably be in Alpha mode too. Dark, territorial, primal Alpha mode - so hot! I quickly don a white lace bra and thong set and throw the sundress on, the material sliding over me with ease. The sundress is a size bigger than when I wore it last, not that I'm complaining, it still flows and hugs my body in all the right places. I quickly throw my hair up in a loose braid, which will most likely fall out if I go swimming tonight. I grab a towel from the hall closet just in case that happens.

Walking down the hall into the living room, Shadow is sprawled out in front of the TV, watching whatever he can manage to find. "Hey Shadow, can you give me a lift to the lake? I'll mind-link with you when I'm ready for you to pick me back up. If that's not too much trouble for you" I wink at him with a smile.

'WOW! You look different, in a good way of course, just different. I-I don't remember when you last wore a dress.' He rambles as he climbs off the couch and heads to the front door. I open the door for us and shut it behind, keeping in mind to not lock it. I climb on his back as we leave the front steps. Normally, I would just walk to the lake, but it's dark and I opted for no footwear, not that I had any that matched my dress.

With Shadow's long strides and speed, we are at the lake within minutes. As I predicted, no one is around. The almost full moon flying high in the sky, glistening in the water below. The birds and crickets are all that can be heard. It's such a magical spot, probably why we came here so often as kids and teens. I climb down off Shadow and land softly in the grass, dropping my towel nearby.

"Thank you for the ride, now scoot...please!" I say to him giving him a kiss on the forehead. He licks my cheek and takes off in the direction we had just come, heading back to Mom and Dad's no doubt. I wait until I know he is gone before walking up to the edge of the lake. Dipping my toes in the water and back out, "holy crap that's cold!" I can fix that... I bend down to the water, dipping my hand in, and closing my eyes.

"Calor..." my hand glows red and starts to warm up the lake. Within seconds the lake is warm enough to go swimming, I take my hand out of the water, looking around again to make sure no one is around before reaching for the shoulder straps of my dress and letting it fall to the ground.

Standing there in my bra and underwear, I bask in the moonlight feeling rejuvenated and feel my powers recharging.

Deep breath...

I can't believe I'm doing this and with him of all people...

Unable to stand the tension within my own body any longer, I step into the water and keep walking until I'm deep enough to shallow dive. The water is just warm enough but still cool enough to give goosebumps; it's perfect for a warm summer night like tonight. I rise to the surface and look back to the bank of the lake and see him standing there, watching me. His eyes are dark mixed with anticipation and hunger; a desire that I haven't seen in him in a long time.

"Couldn't wait for me I see." He calls out as he starts stripping his clothes off slowly. I make my way back towards the bank but stop just enough to be able to have my feet firmly touch the bottom of the lake, the water at my chest. I blush at him standing there as the moonlight reflects off his muscles. I notice him breathing heavily, if I had to guess, he must have run from the pack house in his human form, his wolf form would have destroyed his clothes. He strips his clothing until he is down to his boxers, walking up to the water, "is it warm?"

I smile and shrug, "Don't be a baby, just get in."

He smiles back at me before stepping into that water. That smile of his can break a thousand hearts and let him get away with murder. His smiles, his eyes, his muscles; all give me goose-bumps and heat my core up in ways that they shouldn't. I can't let him affect me like this, well at least I shouldn't, but I have no control over myself. He moans as he sinks deeper into the water and vanishes.

Minutes go by, and I'm just standing there afraid to move, but he hasn't resurfaced. My heart starts to race, and my nerves and body overwhelm me with anticipation as I wait for him. I should have known that he would do this, he used to do this trick when we would come up here as teens. I would always get worked up with him holding his breath for so long.

After what seems like an insanely long time, strong arms wrap around my waist, but instead of pulling me underwater, they pull me up against his warm, firm body. He holds me close and tight as he nuzzles my neck from behind. I moan at the feel of being in his arms, the feel of his five o'clock shadow scraping against my neck, my heat ignites further as he nips lightly along my neckline.

Damn, this feels good…this feels right, and yet it doesn't…

I turn around in his arms, wrapping my arms around his neck, and look up into his dark blue eyes. In a flash, his eyes glow, his wolf acknowledging that he's just as happy to be here with me. Galen leans down, taking full control of my lips. His Alpha aura heightens my own arousal, and my heat roars to life. My grip around his neck tightens as I jump up and wrap my legs around his waist. His arms and hands slide under my legs and ass, supporting my weight with ease. Our kiss deepens, tongues sliding over one another as Galen starts walking us back to the bank. I didn't even realize that we were out of the water until he laid me down on my towel.

His body towering over him, dripping water all over me. "Tsk, tsk, tsk...Really Callie, panties?" he jokes. In a quick tug, a single rip is heard as the flimsy material gives way to his strength as he rips them right off my body and throws them over his shoulder to land in the grass. I just giggle and lay back, watching him watch me with such hunger. I blush as he stands and pulls off his boxers, relieving his rock-hard erection. "See something you want Callie?" He snickers as he wraps his hand around his shaft, his fingertips barely able to touch together.

Unable to speak, I spread my legs nervously. He's too big, I haven't done this in a *loooooong* time. But what's worse is that I do want this. I want him to destroy my body with his. Once we do this, it will cross the line that we've never crossed before, and yet, I am craving to go over that line. He kneels down and crawls between my legs, positioning his erection at the opening of my sex. He looks down at me, locking eyes with me, "Are you sure Callie? Last chance to back out."

I reach between us wrap my hand around his erection and start to stroke him. He growls at the feel of my hands working him up and down slowly, building him up more. "Yes, Galen. I'm sure, I want this. I want you." I say breathlessly. He leans forward and growls in my ear, as he thrusts himself into me in one quick thrust, filling me so completely. The girth of his erection feels like it's splitting my sex open; ripping me apart. The pain slowly turns into a burn as my body attempts to adjust to his size. I yelp at the pain and arch my back from not having intercourse in so long, but he just stays still allowing my body to adjust to his sheer size.

After the pain subsides I nod at him and he starts to rock himself in and out of me slowly, building up a heat between us so fierce. As the intensity builds between us, I wrap my legs around his waist, pulling him in deeper with each thrust. I grip my towel to prevent myself from going over the edge of my climax before him. My body starts to tremble as my orgasm starts to build, I can feel myself float closer and closer to the edge.

"Not yet Callie, not yet...I'm almost there...Wait for me!" He urges breathlessly in tune with his thrusts. He quickens his pace, thrusting harder and deeper. I know I won't last long; a sweat has already started to erupt all over my body. I'm so close to the edge, that I can't bear it for too much longer. I look up into his eyes, they are glowing with this brilliant amber coloring, he's so close to the edge, as is his wolf.

"NOW CALLIE! NOW!" His deep thrust, almost hitting my cervix, is all it takes to send us both tumbling over the edge, our orgasms spilling into each other. I arch my back as his release spills into me. I arch my back as he gives one last thrust before his climax ends and he collapses on me.

He rolls us onto our sides as he slowly withdraws from my sex. My body still fluttering and floating, enjoying my orgasm. He drapes an arm over me, pulling me closer to him, both of us sweating from the cardiac workout. He kisses my forehead as I rest my head against his chest.

We lay there looking up at the stars, just being together, enjoying each other's touch as the aftershocks of our orgasms slowly dissipate. Not going to lie, I've dreamed of this happening with Galen when we were growing up together, but I never thought that it would happen after all this time.

"So that was unexpected..." I break our silence.

"It wasn't for me, I am surprised we hadn't done this as teens. This, here with you right now feels right." His statement hits me hard, am I hearing this right?

"We could have if you weren't chasing every pretty piece of tail in this pack." I retort with a grin, giving his chest a light smack.

"Eh, well I was young a foolish then, what can I say?" He chuckles as he holds me tighter to him. "Stay here with me. Be the next pack Shaman."

"Wh-what? So, is that what this was for you? Pull on my heartstrings for you, use our history, have sex with me, all to get me to say yes to being the pack Shaman?!" I push out of his arms in anger and stand up. Finding my dress and pulling it on in a huff. *'Shadow, come get me. I need you now! This was a mistake!'* I mind-link to Shadow, he doesn't need to answer me to know that he is on his way. He would never leave me alone in any vulnerable situation.

"Callie, wait! That's not what I meant. Well, not all of it really. Just let me explain." Galen gets up after me, throws on his cargo shorts, and grabs my wrist. I turn to face him; my face and body language radiate how pissed off I am. "If you think about it, you would have been the next Shaman anyway, why do you think Maybelle took you under her wing when you were five? Everyone in the pack knew that they wouldn't support you leading this pack, you're not a werewolf. Being the daughter of the Alpha and a witch, it just makes sense with you being the next Shaman."

I refuse to listen to him; I turn away from him trying to find my panties. Shredded or not, I am not about to leave anything behind. He doesn't care about me the way that I thought he did. It's not entirely his fault though, I never should have held a torch for him all these years, even if just a small torch. Spotting my panties a few feet away, I reach down to scoop them up, but Galen gets to them first.

"These are mine!" He states as he shoves the shredded panties in his pants pocket. "Don't you feel it, Callie? We belong together, it just makes sense with me as Alpha and you as the pack Shaman. You belong to me."

"You don't know that, Galen. You could still meet your moon-fated mate someday and then I would be cast aside...again" I say in a low and controlled tone, still unable to meet his gaze as small tears well up in my eyes. I really thought this was something more to him; I had hoped it was something more. Before I can think further on anything, my anger takes over, "ardeat," I say in a hushed voice.

"Ahh!" Galen winces in pain, lets go of my wrist, and pulls his hand back instantly, his palm red from where he had gripped my wrist. I start walking toward the forest, hoping that Shadow will come to my aid. I'm just so upset that I finally got what I had hoped for only to have it be for the wrong reasons. "Callie, the moon Goddess hasn't given me a mate yet, maybe there is a reason why..." Galen starts towards me.

Shadow bursts through the tree line and leaps forward, landing right in between us. He snarls towards Galen in warning, who stops dead in his tracks as I climb on Shadow's back. Without my urging, Shadow takes off into the woods back towards my parent's house, leaving Galen standing there dumbfounded. I could have sworn I heard him say "Don't go", but that could have just been my imagination and hope. Unable to bear it any longer, tears pour down my face as we approach Mom and Dad's. The sooner Shadow and I leave, the better...

Mom and Dad still aren't back yet from their run, the house is as dark as how I left it earlier this evening. I crawl into my bed alone.

My sex sore and reminding me of my mistake.

A mistake I won't make again.

***

The next morning, I wake up early and get a jump start on packing up my Jeep. Shadow and I need to get out of here and just think about everything. Being here is just too hard to say no, I need a clear mind and level head to make any future decisions. Dad helps me load all my weapons and bags silently. Shadow and Mom just sit quietly on the porch. I think everyone is just afraid to say the wrong thing, and sometimes silence is better.

"Honey are you sure..." Mom starts to say.

"Mom, don't. Please. I need to get home. I'm sure my phone is going to blow up with messages the minute of get back to the city. And besides, I've got orders to complete for the full moon parties coming up this week." I just can't deal with her trying to be in my business right now, and I don't need her opinions, not like I ever really listen to them anyway. I close up all the doors on the jeep. "Shadow, you ready?"

He jumps off the porch, bounding over to me with his tail wagging. *'Yeah, I'm happy to go home too buddy. Thanks for not saying anything about last night.'* "How do you want to go home? Travel size or spell-bound?" I ask him out loud; I'm not a fan of mind-linking with him in front of my parents, I find it rude.

'Spell-bound direct to home, please. No need to shrink me down to size just for the drive home. Besides one day you could accidentally get too stuck at that size and then you wouldn't be able to have a trusty steed to rescue you.' He winks at that last comment.

I nod to him, placing my hand on his forehead, and close my eyes. "Revertetur in terram suam," the gold glow radiates out of my hand and wraps around Shadow and within a minute, Shadow disappears.

Sighs...

I turn back toward my parents, and we go in for a big group hug.

"You know you are welcome home anytime kiddo," Dad says warmly. I just nod and pat him on the back.

"Honey, are you going to stop by the pack house and say bye to Alpha Galen?" Mom slips in quickly; she just can't help herself.

I roll my eyes and break away from the hug. "There is nothing left to say, Mom. Last night was a mistake, one that won't be repeated. One that can't be repeated. I've got to go. I'll send a wisp to you when I get home to let you know that I made it safely." I give them each a kiss on the cheek and start to head back towards the Jeep.

A large figure steps out of the forest, catching my attention. I pause, realizing that it's a large grey wolf with minimal red markings. The size of the wolf and its markings, Galen. But he's just standing there watching me leave, not doing anything about it. He takes a step forward, I shake my head, and he stops in his tracks.

"Goodbye, Galen," I whisper so softly, but I know he heard me as he responds with a low whine. I climb into my Jeep, start her up, and take off down the road, leaving pack territory. I look up in my rear-view mirror to see the wolf step out into the middle of the road behind me. The wolf howls a long and sad tune, causing more tears to well up in my eyes again and start to fall down my cheeks.

Nine

I DON'T REALLY KNOW how I got home; my mind was on autopilot until I got through my front door and leaned against it, shutting it closed and locking out the world. I leaned my head back against the door and dropped my bag to the floor. My mind is still reeling from all that has happened over the last 48 hours, trying to figure out where to start.

Deep breath...

'Do you want to talk about what happened last night between you and Alpha Galen?' Shadow's voice startles me, causing me to open my eyes and find him standing in the kitchen.

Shaking my head, "No I don't. We don't really have time for that now anyway." Standing in the kitchen, I pull out my phone and open my Shopify account; along with being a nurse and a witch, I have a Shopify account for my medicinal baked goods and drink packets., anyway

The full moon really boosts my account, as many businesses within the city buy and sell my products at their establishments. Shifters go over the moon for my wolfsbane brownies. Looking at my store account, there are over 200 orders for brownies, cookies, teas, and drink packets. I've never had this many orders to fulfill. Feeling slightly overwhelmed might be a bit of an understatement. "Shadow, I'm going to need your help with all these orders," I inform him, showing the account orders to him.

'Grrrr...'

I just chuckle at his internal groan; with the way he acts, you would think that I was asking him to help me solve world hunger or something just as detrimental to the world. "It's just for a little while Shadow, I'll transform you back as soon as I don't need you anymore, a couple of hours tops." I plead with a big puppy face.

Shadow sighs, 'Okay, fine. Let's get this over with. After though, I want to hear about last night.' His counteroffer is hard to refuse, he is my familiar, and he really should know what's going on, especially when it could involve him later on. I nod in agreement, placing my hand on his forehead.

"Ut homo factus es." My hand emits a bright green glow that surrounds Shadow, so bright that I have to shut my eyes. Within a couple of seconds, the light vanishes, and Shadow is standing there in human form, naked... Well, only part of Shadow is human, the top half; I'm a witch who has been a little frazzled over the last 24 hours, so my spell didn't go perfectly. "Well, that's never happened before, but at least you're able to help me. Just watch your tail." I giggle at the incompleteness of my spell.

Shadow looks over himself, standing on his hind legs, he's human from the waist up and the waist down, he's just his regular wolf self. "Callie, what the hell?!" He stumbles slightly, trying to get used to balancing on just two legs.

"Well, at least you don't have to worry about wearing any pants. Just put an apron on silly; we need to get cracking." I demand as I toss an extra full-length apron his way.

Looking at Shadow, as he puts on the apron, his chest muscle ripped and barely concealed by the apron. I can't help but wonder what it would be like if he were fully human. If his upper body is anything to judge by, he would have to beat women off with a bat. He reminds me of an Ancient Greek statue; perfectly ripped and chiseled, dark brown-almost black hair long enough to braid, deep dark brown eyes, and arms so strong that you almost have to worry about being crushed.

"Shadow, have you ever thought about being human? Like fully human?" My heart starts to race a little, and I flush with embarrassment. I cannot be thinking about him like this; he's my familiar, my protector and guide. He's not a piece of meat or eye candy, at least not for me, anyway.

"No." He responds flatly. "I was human and then I died. The Goddess brought me back to be a familiar for witches to learn from my mistakes. You know this. If I were ever to be human again, I would have no, magic. I would age and die and that would be it."

Way to be Mr. Gloom-and-doom Shadow... I just roll my eyes.

"Why don't you get started on making up the brownies and cookies while I go collect the herbs?" I suggest as I grab my garden basket, gloves, and pruning shears.

Shadow digs out a couple of mixing bowls, some spoons, and the recipe cards and starts to get to work cracking eggs and mixing everything together; more like making a mess as he attempts to help. I chuckle and just leave him to it.

Wolfsbane brownies:
•Peel and mash up 3 bananas
•Combine 2 large eggs with bananas, mix until blended
•Add 1/2 cup of melted butter
•Add 1/2 cup of dark chocolate cocoa powder and 1/4 cup of protein powder - mix well, add a drizzle of water if batter is too thick
•Scoop in 2 cups of peanut butter
•Once mixed thoroughly, add a handful of dark chocolate chips and wolfsbane.
•Transfer to baking pan and bake at 350 degrees for 20-25 minutes

Out in my garden, I set my gloves and shears in my basket placing them on the ground and lifting my hands out to the plants overtaking my garden. I need to come out here and trim some of the babies back... "Excitare hortus." My hands glow an amber color brightly and the magic moves over the garden like a mist. Plants start to untangle and straighten themselves out, flowers and herbs that were sulking over now bloom and erect themselves. So much easier to walk through the garden without tripping over plants.

I walk over to the medicinal section of my garden, medicinal however slightly deadly and dangerous in the wrong amounts. Just a sample of the herbs and flowers in this section of the garden are wolfsbane, foxglove, hemlock, and nightshade; of which all are kept 10 feet away from the other plants in my garden. I've noticed over the years that my other plants and flowers do not grow well if they are planted too close to my medicinal section. This makes sense as I've said before, these can be deadly if not handled properly.

Kneeling on the ground next to the wolfsbane, I notice that this particular plant has grown exponentially since last month. "Hello beautiful," I whisper to it as I examine the flower for pests. I know it sounds crazy, but I swear my plants really do respond to my voice and touch, it's as if they have minds of their own. The leaves and off-shoots of the plant curl around my finger in response to me. I chuckle and smile to myself, "Yes, I missed you too." I grow three different shades of wolfs-bane in my garden, the deeper the color the more potent the flower. After examining a few different stems, I clip a couple of each color, singing to the plants to make them feel loved.

I clip a few extra flowers: deadly nightshade, hemlock, fox-glove, mugwort, lavender, dragon's blood sage, and eucalyp-tus.

With a full basket, I head back inside and see that my kitchen is destroyed. Do you want to know how to piss a witch off? Destroy her kitchen.

I'm not OCD or anything, but my kitchen is my happy place to do spells and create potions with baked goods. Shadow has, without a doubt, destroyed my kitchen. Think of hoarders, well this is just as bad. He managed to get ingredients all over the counter, I was only gone for 10 minutes.

"SHADOW?! What have you done?!" I shout, startling him in the process, causing him to spill more ingredients, as I set my basket on the counter, taking off my gloves.

"You're the one who wanted my help, do you know how hard it is to be on just two wolf legs?" He retorts back, dropping everything on the counter and throwing his hands up in surrender.

Deep breath.

"Just stop! Please. I'll do it, just stop making it worse!" I plead waving my hands at him, anything to get him out of my kitchen. "Derivare ad lupum," I say with no warning to Shadow, my hand glows bright white and Shadow is transformed back to his wolf self. "Just stay out of my kitchen."

'Hmph, that was rude. A little warning before transformation would have been nice.' He leaves the kitchen, trotting down the hallway to his room.

I turn back to the kitchen. Oh, what a mess is an understatement. The only way to get out of this mess is to do a little magic, normally I wouldn't waste any on cleaning my kitchen, but this is just too much for my anxiety to handle alone. Deep breathing my way out of this is just not an option.

I close my eyes and raise my hands, palms facing the mess, "culina mundare." A bright purple glow floats out from my hands and shimmers over my kitchen. The dirty dishes that were on the counter start to move toward the sink, as the faucet turns on the hot water and the sponge moves to the soap dispenser. The sponge gets a glob of soap and moves all over the counter to wipe up the sticky situations.

My kitchen looks like that scene from the original Sleeping Beauty, where the three fairies are cleaning up the house, sewing a dress, and making a cake. Well instead of a cake, I'm making brownies, savory scones, and cookies, if I have enough time and the kitchen is cleaning itself. An apron flies through the air and magically ties itself around my waste.

I pull out my cutting board and mortar and pestle. I grab my basket and organize my plants in a row on the counter, trying to place them in an order of which to crush first. The dark blue wolfsbane will be first as I need it for the brownies and some side orders. I pluck the flowers and place them in the mortar. I take the stems and cut them up and place them in with the flowers. The great thing I love about wolfsbane is that the whole plant gets used, including the stem because the whole plant is toxic. In small doses though, or mixed with baked goods, wolfsbane can subdue certain supernaturals, like shifters, or make them high for a few hours, like vampires.

Thankfully, you can't taste it like some of the other plants in my garden, like poison nettle. That's why wolfsbane is so dangerous because when mixed with other ingredients it becomes tasteless. You could easily overdose on Wolfsbane and never know it. As I'm grinding up the plant into a powder, a dark blue powder.

Wait a second...

This looks similar to that substance that I scraped off Kelly's fingers. Hmm, that's odd. I quickly wipe my hands and grab my phone.

I scroll through finding Forest in my contacts, and a couple of text messages from him that I must have missed while on pack territory. I opened up his texts but did not read his, I feel like there is something going on with that substance I found on the patient's fingers that I should follow up on.

Me: Hey Forest, did Forensics come back on that powder yet?

Forest: Hey girl, where have you been?

No, they haven't gotten through all your specimens yet, why?

Well, I know this sounds really silly and probably coincidental, but I'm fulfilling my full-moon orders ready and when I was grinding up the wolfsbane, I noticed that it turns into a blue powder, and it reminded me of the powder I collected off that patient's fingers a couple of days ago.

Sounds silly, right?

No, it doesn't sound silly. Trust your gut Callie.

If you can get me a sample of your wolfsbane, I can bring it to Forensics to take a look at it to see if they are the same or similar.

Sure, I'll save you some. I have to head into the city later to do my deliveries. I could meet you at the Apothecary Cafe, that's my last stop typically.

Sounds great! Gives me time to go home shower and change. Would 7 pm be alright with you?

Yep that works.

It's a date ;)

A date? Umm, ok. See you then :)

Out of nowhere, butterflies fill my stomach and my heart starts to race.

Did I read that right? I have a date. With Forest?

I mean I guess that's not unheard of; I just haven't had a date in a few years, most guys get intimidated when your familiar is the size of a small horse and with teeth and aggression worse than a shark; never mind the fact that I'm one of the most powerful witches within a few hundred miles.

'*Shadow, I don't need your help tonight. I'm going out after I do my deliveries.*' Mind-linking saves time and it's not something he can ignore or say that he didn't hear me tell him.

No longer feeling overwhelmed about all the orders, I turn on my iTunes and play my baking playlist, and just get sucked into the music. Did I mention that baking is my happy place? I've used this brownie recipe so many times that I don't even have to look at the recipe card anymore. I've made it without the wolfsbane, and it makes a fabulous dessert with a scoop of ice cream. I scoop out a small amount of the powder out of the mortar and seal it in a small ziplock bag for Forest.

I grab a big mixing bowl and a whisk and start placing ingredients into the bowl. "Confundo," waving my fingers over the bowl and whisk. The whisk floats off the counter and starts to mix the ingredients in the bowl together as I continue to add more ingredients. I preheat the oven before adding the wolfsbane to the mixture. Once the recipe is nice and smooth looking, I wave my hands at the bowl, "finis," and the whisk stills within the bowl. I pour the mixture into the baking pans and continue this pattern until I have 10 pans filled.

While baking, I work on the other orders that need to be filled. There are many teas and powders to mix up for alcoholic drinks and coffees, special orders for Dark Illusion. I've been doing this little side business for a few years now, and it's been growing steadily every month as word gets out about my baked goods and herbal drink packets. My main contributors are Dark Illusion, Blue Lantern Bar, and the Apothecary Cafe. I do supply a few straggles of people who don't wish to visit those establishments, but I just do porch drop-offs for them. This isn't something I can do full-time just yet, and I'm not sure I would want to either, I enjoy being a nurse and helping people.

I don't know how I've managed it all, but after a few hours of work in my kitchen, I have completed all the orders and restocked some of my powders needed for spells and potions. I start organizing and packaging up the orders into their cute little boxes and ziplocks. I hear Shadow's claws on the hardwood floor before he comes into the kitchen.

'Did you many any extra brownies?' He inquires. *'And why don't you need my help tonight?'*

"Yes, I did make you some brownies." Lifting the lid to a Rubbermaid container, revealing a whole load of extra brownies. "You just need to be careful. This batch came out very potent, no need for you to be drowsy for too long." He jumps up, his front paws on the counter nudging the lid open and grabbing a brownie. "Hey!" I yell at him, swatting his nose with a towel. He scampers back down the hallway to his room with a huge brownie half-hanging out of his mouth. I just stand there and shake my head at him.

I don't mind him eating the brownies; however, his reaction time is definitely hindered if he eats too many. Personally, I think he just likes to eat them all because then I don't get to, he acts like such a child sometimes. The brownies help me with my anxiety sometimes, the wolfsbane and chocolate help take the edge off after a long day at work. Working as a nurse has its perks, but the stress that comes with helping patients and their families can be a bit much sometimes. That's when I go for a brownie.

The difference between Shadow having those brownies versus werewolves having them is that the brownies help the werewolves in a way that prevents them from shifting and turning savage. Most werewolves go shift and hunt or run with their pack in the woods during a full moon, however, if you aren't part of the pack and pledge allegiance towards the Alpha then you don't get to go into the woods. It's that way for a lot of shifters during a full moon, be part of a pack and go hunt, or take your chances alone and find ways to deal with the full moon frenzy. With the number of shifters in Capital City, there would be massacres every month like there used to be before the treaty between the supernaturals.

Shifters aren't the only ones who are affected by the full moon. Vampires can't hide their true form during a full moon and become angrier, and more territorial, which is why many of them seek out wolfsbane, of some form, to get high and keep themselves from going over the edge. Thankfully, wolfsbane doesn't affect witches, well most witches, as I've said before I'm special thanks to my parents for being werewolves. I wouldn't say I'm a hybrid because I have no wolf to shift into; however, Shadow says that could still happen, I'm not holding my breath for that though. I don't think I could handle being a hybrid.

Looking at all my orders on the counter, I worry if I've made enough to satisfy all the customers. With my orders increasing every month, if I'm not careful I'm going to need to get some help that can ACTUALLY help me in the kitchen, unlike Shadow.

"Shadow, I'm going to load up the Jeep and shower before heading into the city." I call out to him, "I'm also going to be home late tonight, so you're on your own."

'Why are you going to be home late tonight, Callie?' He says, startling me. I turn around and there he is sitting in the hallway. He was so quiet just now that it was a little eerie.

"Forest and I are meeting up for coffee after I drop off the deliveries." I grab a pile of the orders and bring them out to the jeep, taking notice of the peculiar warm weather.

Maybe I'll wear my dark blue sundress and flats tonight. Shadow is still sitting there in the kitchen when I come back in like he's waiting to finish the conversation or something. "What?"

"Shadow enough! What happened last night with Alpha Galen made me feel amazing, it's the same connection we had when before we left. It's still there between him and me. But he knew that and used it against me. He made me vulnerable for just a brief moment and then ruined it all with pack bullshit, without even a second thought. The pack will always come first to him. I want someone to put me first." I huff out my explanation.

Last night with Galen was beautiful and earth-shattering, but it was also a mistake. One that I wish I could experience again with him without any pack drama going on. "Besides I need to get a sample of the wolfsbane to Forest, it reminded me of the substance I found on my patient the other day. He's going to give it to Forensics."

'Maybe you should have told ALL that to Alpha Galen? Maybe things would be different?' Shadow retorts and starts to walk back to his room. He turns to look back at me, *'And for what it's worth Callie, I've always put you first...'*

"Shadow, I'm sorry. I didn't mean to blow up at you." I start walking toward him and he turns away from me.

'I think you are wrong, but you do whatever makes you happy. I can't stop you, I'm JUST your familiar.' He states coldly before

going to his room. I would have followed after him, but it's no use. He's right to an extent, I do need to have a conversation with Galen. Just not tonight.

I make two more trips out to the jeep with my orders. Thinking about my date with Forest has my stomach all knotted up and my body flushed. I'm going on a date. I haven't been on a date in a long time.

This will be good for me.

I refuse to let the last 24 hours mess with my headspace because I'm going on a date.

A date with Forest.

Ten

ARRIVING AT DARK ILLUSION is my second-to-last stop for deliveries. Normally, I would just spell-cast my order to a specific location, but the owner here really doesn't like "things" or "people" just popping in without notice. Dark Illusion is one of the few establishments within Capitol City that is friendly towards supernaturals.

The establishment is part bar and nightclub, with a full restaurant and hotel attached. The owner, Max Roberge, wanted to build a place for all supernaturals to feel safe at all times. So much so that he created his own protection spell that prohibits magic being used, other than his, while on the property. Which is why I can't spell-cast my order into the kitchen directly.

I'm not sure what kind of supernatural Max is, or even how old he is, but he has the ability to spell-craft to some degree. I know he can't make potions or magical baked goods though, that's why he buys them from me at a discounted price. In return, I get access to the nightclub and bar any time I want to with no cover charge.

Johnny, the doorman, sees me coming down the sidewalk with an armful of goodies. "Good evening, Miss Spellcaster," he says with a smile, opening the door for me. Johnny may look old, but I've seen him rough up customers, much younger and bigger than him, who needed it. "Do you need any help?"

"Just the door, as always Johnny. Thank you." I smile back at him, stepping into the lobby.

I'm always mystified by how bright and colorful the lobby is. Light fixtures on the walls and hanging from the ceiling give off a vibrant glow, you wouldn't know that it was after-dark already. My wedge sandals make a small clunking on the tiled floor. I'm not the most graceful in wedges, but they go with my dark navy sundress better than my boots.

I walk up to the counter of the concierge desk, "Can you please let Max know that I'm here with his delivery?" I ask the young man working behind the counter.

"Ummm. Deliveries are made on the loading dock out back." He states rudely, without looking up from his computer.

I set my order on the counter, reaching out with my magic, and find that this young man is human. There is no vibration of magic in him at all. Does he even know what goes on in this place?

I ask again, politely and with a smile, "Can you please call Max? He's expecting me." I'm trying so hard to not lose my temper or control over my magic, wouldn't want to take a chance of ruining my hair and make-up before my date.

"Like I said before ma'am, deliveries are completed out back," he states and goes about his business.

"Can you just call…"

"No! I'm not calling the owner. Do you know how many people claim they know the owner?! As I've said, deliveries are brought out back on the loading dock." He repeats and ignores me.

I stand there slightly dumbfounded, I mean I guess he has a point. I reach into my bag and grab my cell phone. I scroll through my contacts and click on Max.

"Good evening Calista. What is the pleasure of your call this *fiiiine* evening?" A deep sexy voice answers, one that can only belong to Max.

"Hi Max, I'm trying to drop off my delivery, but your concierge won't take my order. And he wouldn't call you either." I say loud enough over the phone for the young man to hear as well.

"Oh hell, he must be the new one. I'll be right down in a minute." He hangs up before I can say another word.

I stuff my phone back in my bag and turn towards the young man with a smile. Jokes on you buddy. I don't envy you after this, crossing paths on the wrong side of Max never ends well for anyone.

"Calista, I apologize for this wait," that sexy voice fills the lobby from the elevator. Max comes out, arms open and a huge smile on his face.

If I had to guess, Max is about 6'8", weighing probably close to 250 lbs, all of which is muscle. This man is seriously fit and jacked. Between that and his long brown hair, bright silver eyes, and trimmed beard, the dude is a knock-out. I enter his embrace, he radiates heat like a shifter but doesn't smell like one, and we exchange a kiss on the cheek.

"It's really no problem at all Max, I just wanted to make sure that you got the delivery," I say as I pat the side of the boxes. "Your order was larger this month, so I didn't want it to get lost or damaged. I also threw in some extra wolfsbane and hemlock powder packets to add to mixed drinks for the bar as well."

"Oh, Dizzy will be so thrilled by this, she says that those powders are great in her mixed cocktails. Thank you so much!" Max snaps his fingers at this concierge, "Roger, take the box to the kitchen. Make sure the chef and Dizzy know about the deliveries, they both know what to do." His voice stern toward the man. "Oh, and Roger, next time Miss Spellcaster here drops her delivery off, you'll take it right away without any issues. Or you'll become an issue. Got it?"

Roger doesn't miss a beat, he nods nervously toward Max, grabs the heavy boxes, and scurries out back to the kitchen. My attention returns towards Max, who's leaning against the counter, "Max, I think you made him piss himself with fright." I giggle a little bit.

Max turns towards me and leans forward, "My dear Calista, we miss seeing you here. Many of the regular hotties, in the club, have been asking for you. You're not turning tricks, are you?"

Rolling my eyes and blushing, "No Max, I'm not turning tricks as you put it. I've just been busy; you know the usual. And now I'm getting roped into the pack business. I promise I'll make a visit soon."

"Well, you better. Stress is just radiating out of your aura dear; you need to take a break and recharge. Your aura isn't as shiny as it normally is." He pouts as he fusses with the floral arrangement on the counter.

"I know, I know. When I'm back to work tomorrow, I'll ask Brody when we are coming back. I promise." Giving in under pressure, and throwing my hands up in surrender, puts a huge smile on Max's face.

"Good. I'll hold you to it." Max gets a ding on his phone, "Ok dear, I need to go it put another fire. You call me and let me know when you are coming. Caio!" He dismisses me while texting angrily back on his cell phone, walking away in a hurry.

Roger reappears with my empty delivery boxes and places them on the counter. "Thank you, Roger," I say with another smile taking the boxes with me. He just nods and returns to his work, a little paler too.

Leaving Dark Illusion, Johnny grabs the door for me again, "Have a good evening, Miss Spellcaster."

"Thank you, Johnny. You, too." I make my way to my Jeep and head towards the Apothecary Cafe.

***

Rain starts lightly tapping on my windshield as I pull into the parking lot behind the cafe. The cafe is so small that I always park out back when I make deliveries. Madge, the owner, an older woman and were-panther is out back holding the door open for me. She must have seen me pulling in.

I scoop up my boxes and dash to the door, attempting to stay dry. Madge has been running the cafe for over a hundred years and when I opened my Shopify account, she became my first regular customer. I always bring her extra goodies for no extra charge, what's good for her business is good for Capital City and its inhabitants.

She greets me with a smile, "Good evening, Callie. Well, don't you look spectacular this evening." She takes the heavy boxes from me with ease.

"Aww, thank you, Madge. I actually have a date tonight..." blushing as I whisper that last part as if saying it too loud will jinx it all.

"That's wonderful! It wouldn't happen to be with one of Capital City's finest officers, would it?" She inquires. My only response is to blush profusely. "It's about time that you two went out, you're always hanging out and working in the hospital together."

"He isn't here already, is he?"

Madge nods as she starts to unpack and organize the delivery. I quickly scoot over to the nearest reflective surface, an antique baking sheet hanging on the wall, to check myself over. Running my fingers through my hair and quickly adding some lightly tinted chapstick.

"You look great dear. Stop fidgeting and relax. You deserve a night out; have a good time." Madge encourages me through the kitchen and down the hallway leading to the front area of the cafe.

Looking out to the front of the cafe, the decor is an earth-toned base with deep rich colors in the furniture, some candles are lit on the tables to give off a soft glow. There is a fireplace blazing, multiple deep-cushioned, dark-colored lounge chairs and couches circling the fireplace, and a small table with chairs scattered around. It's a very relaxed environment and offers a great place for people to date or unwind from a long day, or just a great space to start your day off right.

There is he.

Forest managed to grab a table by the window, looking out the window as the rain started to pick up. He's even more handsome just sitting there, sipping on a cup of coffee without a care in the world. His tall muscular form seems out of place in such a small, more private setting. Give that man credit though, he's wearing my favorite type of outfit; relaxed-fitted dark blue jeans, a tight black fitted tee shirt, with an earth-toned plaid flannel, and his usual black hiking boots. Absolutely mouth-watering.

Deep breath...

As I approach the table, I notice that he's already ordered for me, looks like hot cocoa and double chocolate biscotti...my favorite! That man knows me so well. "Hi Forest," I say softly so, as to not disturb others in the cafe.

He turns his gaze from the window abruptly, looks up at me, and smiles. He gets up from his seat to greet me, placing his hands on the small of my back and kissing my cheek at the same time. "You are so beautiful," he whispers in my ear, his lips slightly caressing my ear. I blush so easily as his natural scent of coffee fills my senses.

He walks around me and pulls my chair out for me. "Thank you," I say as I sit down, draping my bag across the back of my seat.

Forest walks back and sits in his chair across from me. He picks up his coffee and takes a sip, all without losing my eye contact. "You made good time, looks like the weather is picking up out there." Following his gaze out the window, the rain continues and thunder and lighting started to rumble. I turn my attention back to him, his stare burning right through me, goosebumps erupting over my skin and making me blush simultaneously.

I bring the drink he's ordered for me to my lips; the deep chocolate tingles my tongue and nose, filling me up with the rich flavor. The hot chocolate already burning within my core. There is something different about this hot chocolate, a subtle taste of something else, something earthy.

Hazelnut? Chicory?

I shrug it off, no need to get paranoid and start dissecting every little thing. The biscotti is perfect with my hot chocolate; chocolate with dark chocolate chunks is pure heaven in my mouth.

He watches me just enjoy all the chocolaty goodness and just smiles. "What? Do I have something on my face?" I ask in a panic.

"No, you're perfect. I'm just surprised it's taken us this long to set this up. I've been wanting to ask you out for a while, just wasn't sure how to go about it" He admits.

"You and I have hung out numerous times, asking me out should have been easy." I tease as I take another bite of the biscotti.

What is going on with the men in my life? First Galen, now Forest. This full moon has men acting horn-crazed.

Forest remains quiet, drinking his coffee, and making eyes at me. I return his gaze and just start talking about all the things as if this wasn't our first date. Conversations with Forest have always been easy, I feel so relaxed and comfortable talking with him, so much that I forget that we are on a date. Madge occasionally walks over to check in on us, refilling our cups as needed. I keep meaning to ask her about the flavor of the hot chocolate, but I get distracted by our date. It's not until 3 cups later that I start to feel jittery, my inner desire is blazing, and I start to shift more in my seat. I feel as if I'm burning up, my core is blazing.

"If you'll excuse me just a second." I smile at him as I get up from the table and go to leave for the bathroom.

"Don't be gone for too long." His deep voice slithers through me and adds to my already blazing heat. I smile back at him, my face permanently flushed from all the hot chocolate and desire coursing through my body.

I step into the bathroom, thankful that it's a single-room-style bathroom, large enough for me to pace around. Looking in the mirror while washing my hands, my face is beet red. I grab a paper towel, wet it with some cold water, and wipe it down my forehead and back of my neck. My stomach is jumping all over the place and my heart is racing.

I need to calm down before I go back out there...
It's just Forest, this is not a big deal...
Did I eat or drink something?
Did I have too much?
It's just hot chocolate and biscotti, I'm being ridiculous.

After a few minutes, I leave the bathroom and bump right into a large, rock-solid form. I brush my bangs behind my ear and see that I've bumped into Forest. Startled and slightly alarmed, "Something wrong Forest?"

His hands grip my upper arms and pushes me back against the door of the bathroom. Unmoving his hands, he leans forward as if he's going to kiss me, just before his lips touch mine, "You took too long," he whispers and then crashes his lips on mine hard. My mouth instinctively opens as his tongue fiercely takes control and wanting to explore.

My body explodes with my heat and desire, my head spinning, my hands grabbing onto his arms as our kiss deepens. Forest lets go of my left arm and fiddles with the bathroom doorknob, causing us to almost fall to the floor as the door springs open from him pressing me up against it. He pushes me up against the counter and breaks our kiss briefly, looking at me with dilated eyes. Dark predatory eyes and I'm the prize.

"You don't allow this, only I do." His tone is deep and heavy with lust. His lips hard against me once again, his tongue possessing mine, pushing his body firmly against me. I can feel his erection straining through his jeans. I go to reach up to wrap my hands and arms around his neck, he quickly grabs my wrists and pin them behind my back, my head still spinning. "Relax, just go with it, princess. Don't fight this."

I can feel something is wrong, my head is spinning more than just with lust, sweat beading along the back of my neck, my heart is racing too fast, and I can feel my heat and desire exploding, wanting more and more.

Too hot, I'm too hot. I can't breathe, I can't think...

Forest continues to kiss me, keeping me pinned between him and the counter, my wrists gripped hard behind my back, unable to break free; he takes one of his legs and moves it between my legs, moving and grinding his leg up against my sex and clit sending tingling throughout my body, causing me to shake.

Moisture starts collecting within my sex and starts to drip into my underwear. He moves his leg harder and faster, my head spinning as he breaks from our kiss and starts to kiss my neck, taking a free hand to grab my breast hard through my dress. I moan at the feel of Forest possessing my body, bringing it to life in a way that is different from that of Galen.

I'm so caught up in the moment that I don't notice that Forest has stopped moving his leg between mine and has moved his free hand under my dress, dragging his hand slowly up my inner thigh. He cups my sex, feeling my moisture leak "I think we should take care of this, don't you?" He snickers, moving my panties to the sides and lightly caressing my wet sex. I spread my legs further apart, granting him further access. He whispers into my ear, "Tell me you want this as much as I do. Tell me that you need this. Tell me that you want me, princess." He teases my sex with his fingers and starts nuzzling against my neck. His hot breath on my neck, his touch on my skin, my head spinning, I can't even form words to answer his questions.

I should be able to answer him, but something doesn't feel right.

What's wrong with me?

Before I can grasp any coherent thought, Forest thrusts two of his fingers deep into my sex. My moan is muffled as Forest possesses my mouth again with his, causing my body to be overwhelmed by both attacks. He starts to piston his fingers in and out of my sex, my body responding to his touch, feeling as if I'm going to explode right there.

He groans as his erection hardens even more, I can feel it growing, I reach out with my magic and can feel his need for more. "Uh-uh, I can feel you reaching around. That's going to cost you, princess!" He reprimands me and thrusts his fingers harder, faster, and deeper into me, causing my body to buck against him as if I have no control over myself. I can feel myself getting closer and closer to the cliff of my climax.

Knock...knock...knock...

Forest freezes with his fingers still inside me, soaked and dripping down his hand. I'm breathing heavily, with this deep ache as my body reels back from the cliff of my climax slowly.

"Callie, is Forest in there with you by any chance? His Captain is on the phone needing him to come back to work." Madge says through the door.

Ugh...

"Yes, Madge I'm in here. Just give me a minute, I'll be right out", he replies withdrawing his fingers from my sex and letting go of my wrists, his disappointment and frustration more obvious than the erection in his pants. "Guess we can always try another time. Maybe next time we'll get to finish our fun." He steps away from me and goes to the sink and washes his hands. "You'll feel better in a little bit. I'll text you later." He kisses my cheek and walks out of the bathroom.

What does he mean that I'll feel better in a bit?

What is going on with me?

I can see Madge standing there holding the phone for him, which he takes and starts talking on as he walks down the hallway. "Are you ok, Callie? You don't look so good" Madge's concern snaps me back to reality. I just nod at her absentmindedly, extremely confused at what just happened.

The bathroom door closes once more, I reach underneath my dress, fix my panties, and straighten myself back. I turn around and see what Madge is talking about, my hair is a mess, my face is flushed, my dress is pulled down revealing my bra for all to see, and there is some discoloration of sorts on my neck. I take a wet paper towel and wipe away the residue.

What the hell just happened?

Eleven

T HE LAST PERSON I expected to see this evening was him. My mind and body were already overwhelmed by my interrupted date with Forest. But there he is, sitting at my kitchen table talking with Shadow. Wearing his usual dark blue jeans and a black tee shirt, that is obviously a size or two smaller than him, he's just sitting there so calmly and smiling, it's almost eerie.

"Galen?" The anticipation flares through my already hormone-crazed body.

"I'll just leave you two be." Shadow excuses himself and goes back to his room, looking up at me as he leaves. *'Be nice.'* He closes the mind-link as he shuts his door.

I set my bag down on the counter, "Can I get you something to drink? I know I need something after tonight." I ask Galen as nicely as I can be. Seeing him sitting there stokes my internal fire that didn't get satiated earlier this evening.

"Water is fine," Galen replies, his voice low and deep as always. He shifts in his seat, the chair squeaking with his movements. I grab a couple of glasses from the cupboard and fill them with water from my countertop berkey setup. As soon as I set a glass in front of him, Galen immediately grabs the glass and downs half the contents within just a breath. I take a seat nervously next to him at the table.

"So..."

"So..."

We both start at the same time. I blush and giggle, I don't know what's gotten into me tonight. "You go first," I tell him and then take a sip of my water.

"I, uh, just wanted to check in on you after you left. What happened at the lake..."

"Was a mistake!" I interrupt him.

"You think it was a mistake?" He growls at me, gripping his glass harder, knuckles turning white. He takes a drink out of his glass and finishes the rest of his water.

"Yes." I look up at him meeting his gaze, eyes glowing as he is doing everything to maintain control over himself. I reach forward and take his empty glass, "here let me get you some more water."

Right as I get up, he grabs my wrist. His hand on my skin, hot, causing me to blush and forces me to turn towards him. He grabs the glass out of my hand and sets it back on the table.

Galen stands up, sliding his body up against mine, he's radiating heat like there is no tomorrow, sliding his hands up my arms, resting his hands on my shoulders, and then back down around my waist. My core rages with fire and heat, my desire erupting through my body. I'm sure he can smell my lust; it doesn't help that Forest and I were interrupted earlier, so my lust is easily ignited. The downfall to having werewolf parents is that my libido is very hard to satiate. Galen sniffs my hair, taking in my scent, my heat, and my desire for more.

"Agh." He jerks back, looking down at me angrily. "Who were you out with tonight? You don't smell like your usual floral self. I DEMAND TO KNOW WHERE YOU WERE AND WHO YOU WERE WITH!"

Ugh...Alphas!

I push away from him, and he grabs both of my upper arms with his huge hands, squeezing hard enough to leave bruises.

I struggle against his grip, jerking my arms a few times, just to confirm my suspicions that he's not letting go anytime soon.

"Who I was with is none of your business. I don't owe you any explanations, Galen! Stop acting like I'm yours!" I shout back as I continue to try to wiggle away and fail.

"Who Callie? Who touched ?!" He demands.

"Alight, geez. I was on a date with Forest. Happy now?" I glare at him fiercely.

Grrrr... He growls deeply. "And how is good ol' Forest? Was he able to seal the deal?" He's so full of anger that I just want to punch him.

"It's none of your business if he did or didn't 'seal the deal'...But if you must know, we were interrupted before we could finish." I reply as I throw my own anger back at him. I surprise him with my answer that I am able to rip my arms out of his grasp, his eyes glowing as he struggles to maintain control.

I look away, and he grabs my chin, pulling my attention and gaze back to him. His lips crash into me, his tongue dives into my mouth taking further possession of me. His hands move to the small of my back, holding my body close to his. My desire takes over, my hands go for his chest, his muscles hard underneath his thin shirt. Our kiss deepens, tongues sliding over each other, the fire deep within me blazing throughout my whole body.

Galen abruptly pulls away, looking at me with lust in his eyes. "Does this feel like a mistake, Callie?" His tone is deep and serious; his question throws me off, my mind spinning from our kiss. His hand wanders underneath my dress, sliding up my thigh, slowly. Goosebumps and shivers tingle over my whole body, pressure building deep inside me, wanting and waiting to explode. I look up into his eyes, glowing back down at me, solid gold.

"I-I don't..." I'm speechless looking up into his golden eyes, getting lost in them, feeling like they are looking into my soul.

"Does it Callie? Tell me to stop and I'll walk away." He pushes his Alpha aura over me, his musky scent of pine trees invading my senses, causing me to forget about what happened at the lake, his hand unmoving from the small of my back applies more pressure as I attempt to struggle free.

Just briefly, I hesitate in my response. I put. With my hands on his chest and attempt to push him away; he moves one of his hands to the small of my back, preventing me from having any space. "We can't..." I'm breathless and all sorts of confused; I look away.

"We can! I didn't just come here to apologize for what happened at the lake, you know." He interrupts and shocks me with his words. "Callie, listen to me, please..." He whispers close to my lips.

I shake my head, trying to clear my mind and body of his scent, his power, and his touch. "Nothing's changed between us." There's obviously something going on between us; I know there is, I can feel it deep down inside.

Before I can utter a single word or form a single thought of reason to tell him to leave, he picks me up and throws me up over his massive shoulder as if I were weightless and starts walking toward my room.

"Galen! Put me down! This! Instant!" I shout as I kick and pound at him.

SMACK!

His large hand hits my ass hard; heat and pain are felt simultaneously as he removes his hand away from my ass.

Oh, my...

I stop fighting him, the pain from the smack has shifted to a warm tingling sensation on my ass, causing my sex to soak through my panties. Truth be told, I was already soaked the minute I saw him in my house, the smack on my ass just intensified it.

"Don't fight this Callie. I can smell your arousal." He kicks my bedroom door open and crosses my room with just a couple of strides. He reaches up under my dress and rips off my panties before throwing me onto my bed. I land hard on my back, and my dress flies up, exposing my thighs and my wet sex. I go to pull down my dress...

"Don't you dare!" He demands, his Alpha aura slams into me, his eyes golden, and his wolf side has taken over. I'm not completely stupid to piss him off when his wolf takes over, there's no reasoning with a shifter when they get to this point. He just stands there, looking down at me, breathing heavily, taking in my nakedness, fighting for control.

"Do you see what you do to me, Callie?" He growls at me.

"No, Galen, I don't see. Why don't you show me?" I know I'm playing with fire at this point. Baiting him isn't the smartest choice I'm making; I want to see if he will finish what he started tonight.

"Don't bait me, baby girl..." He says as he rips off his shirt, grabbing both sides of his chest, the material shredding off him from his strength.

From this angle, he looks like a giant inside my small room. My view wanders down to the bulge in his jeans, his erection straining against the denim. "See something you want?" He arches his eyebrow at me.

"Not yet," I smirk. I spread my legs, showing off my wet sex with the hope of pushing him over the edge, baiting him further.

Grrrr, Galen's growl is low and deep.

"See something you like, Galen?" I ask with a coy smile. He rips his zipper down and his erection springs out of his pants, hard and ready. He grabs my ankles, dragging me so that my ass and sex are on the edge of the bed. He leans over me, holding his erection at the opening of my sex, waiting.

"Same rules apply Callie. I NEED you to tell me what you want." He instructs me with heavy breaths and eyes locked in with mine.

"Galen, if you don't fuck me this instant..." I start to say but am interrupted as Galen slams his erection hard and deep into my sex. I arch my back at the sudden invasion and instant pleasure and warm burn feeling Galen over me and thrusting into me harder and deeper than before.

He grips my hips hard, breathing hard as he thrusts into me, going deeper than he did at the lake. The pressure builds with each thrust, my body flushes as my body comes alive, quickly bringing me closer to the edge of my climax.

"Callie, you're mine...You hear me? You're...mine..." he grunts and growls between thrusts. "Be...my...mate...Callie..."

My head spinning, my body floating; I can't think as my body and soul unravel underneath him. I grip at my comforter, arching my back, my climax building, almost taking over, unable to hold on anymore.

"GALEN!" My world unravels.

He thrusts harder, feeling my climax tear through my body, and pushes him to his climax. His climax spills into my body, and his grip tightens, leaving marks on my skin. My body shudders as I start to come down. Breathing heavily, Galen withdraws himself from my sex and climbs into bed night beside me. My bed groans under his weight, he reaches up and scoops me up around my waist, pulling me towards him.

His warmth sends goosebumps over my skin as I lay my head against his chest, his heartbeat hammering fast. I close my eyes for just a moment, feeling safe and sore at the same time, even if just for a moment.

Is this how it is going to be?

At the hospital?

With the pack?

Would it be like this all the time with him?

"You're overthinking again baby girl…" He whispers to me as he starts to play with my hair.

I groan, lifting my head off his chest and prop myself up on one elbow, looking at him. His eyes are back to normal now, a brilliant blue, a never-ending ocean of blue. "You never answered my question."

"I didn't realize that you asked me one," I smile, knowing what he really wants, well I know what Alpha Galen wants, but I want to know what Galen wants.

He rolls onto his side, facing me, one arm propping him up and resting his hand on my lower abdomen. "Callie, don't play games. You know what I want."

"I know what *Alpha Galen* wants; he wants what is best for the pack. But what does *Galen* want? I NEED to hear you actually say it. Same rules apply." I throw his own rule back in his face with a smile.

He just stares at me, looking into my eyes.

Neither one of us say anything.

I don't know how long we stayed like this, laying partially naked on my bed, just looking at each other.

He breaks the silence, "I want you, Callie." His voice is very soft and quiet, I almost didn't hear him say anything. "I have feelings for you. I always have and when you left the pack all those years ago, it destroyed me…I-I truly believe that you are my moon-fated mate Callie." His confession knocks me over. I hear his words but stare at him in disbelief.

"How do you see this working out?" I'm trying to keep an open mind about all this, I really am, but I have many reservations and a lot of it stems from his Alpha alter ego.

"I don't know. I want you to come back to the pack. But I know that you have built a life away from it… I helped you do it after all, by getting you into nursing school and getting you a job at the hospital. I respect the fact that you have taken your nursing career to the next level and for completing SANE certification. And I respect the fact that you have grown as a witch and a woman. You're beautiful and have so much to offer. I want to be part of your life." His declaration throws me. I never knew how he truly felt until now, and now I don't know what to say.

"The pack chose you as their Alpha. I was forced out after you took over for my Dad. We've been over this a thousand times." Feeling frustrated, I climb out of bed, strip off my dress, and throw on a robe. The soft material provides little comfort, but at least I'm not naked and vulnerable in front of him anymore.

"Hey, don't get mad at me now. You asked a question, and I'm trying to answer it. We can figure something out; you just have to give me a chance and time. Please..." He pleads, not just with his voice, but with his eyes.

Unable to talk about this anymore, I walk out of my room and pound on Shadow's bedroom door. "Shadow, I'm hungry! You want pancakes and bacon?" I yell through his door.

"You're not going to kick me out?" Galen asks.

Shadow's door opens, sticking his head out, *'Dude, she is asking if you want breakfast. Just shut up and accept the meal. You two can figure the rest out later.'* He trots out of his room down the hallway, heading to the kitchen.

I chuckle to myself and follow Shadow to the kitchen, leaving Galen to follow. Being in the kitchen, the silence is awkward. I reach for my phone and play some upbeat music; first up on the playlist: Give 'em Hell by Everybody Loves an Outlaw.

Galen comes up behind me, wrapping his arms around my waist. He kisses the left side of my neck, "Do you need any help?" Pulling me lightly up against his bare chest.

I swat at his hands, "No, I got this. Go sit. Coffee? Tea?" Blushing immensely that he's here in my kitchen and none of us had slept yet.

"Witch's choice." He slaps my ass playfully before leaving the kitchen and taking a seat at the kitchen table, the same spot he sat in last night.

I grab the kettle off the stove, filling it up with water before setting it back on the stove to heat up. I grab a couple of mugs out of the cupboard and get tea from the canister while waiting for the water to boil.

Is this what our future would look like?

I pull out my large mixing bowl, whisk, and all the pancake ingredients. "I hope you like blueberry pancakes," I shout out to the two of them. I wave my hands, and close my eyes, "Misce pancakes." My hands glow a bright yellow color and shimmer over the counter. Measuring cups start to fly through the air, scooping out ingredients and dumping them into a bowl. I start to warm up the griddle on the stove and start cooking up the bacon. I set my oven to warm to keep all the food from getting cold until we could eat.

Is this what it is for normal people the morning after great sex?

Lost in my own thoughts and listening to the music, I hear mumbling going on between Shadow and Galen. Turning to them, "Anything worth sharing?" The kettle on the stove starts whistling, I fill up our mugs and bring them to the table, setting Galen's down in front of him.

"Er, we're just discussing pack business. Thank you." He says taking the mug from me. I take a sip of my tea, before heading back to the kitchen and get working on the pancakes.

I don't know about other witches, but being in my kitchen, listening to music, I get lost in so many thoughts while time just passes quickly. Before I know it, all the bacon and pancakes are cooked up and plated. I dissipate the spells in the kitchen and bring all the food to the table.

Galen and Shadow sit in silence as I drop plates of food underneath their watering mouths. I sit down right next to Galen,

Shadow to my left sitting on the floor, both looking at me, waiting. "Well eat!" I demand waving my hands at them. They both dig into their meals simultaneously; I take another sip of my tea before doing the same.

Breakfast is quiet, minus the loud chomping noises from Shadow. "So, what pack business were you two discussing?" I ask, breaking up the noises. Both pause mid-chew and swallow, taking a moment to look at each other as if asking each other what they should tell me.

"Well, I originally came over last night to talk to you about Maybelle. She's getting worse and I was thinking maybe Shadow here could help Ajax with some minor things. Shadow has trained 3 witches, including you; with his knowledgable background..." Galen starts to explain, but I stop him holding up my hand, stopping him mid-sentence.

"Shadow is my familiar. How am I supposed to do any complicated spells without him?" I ask plainly. "I'm trying to keep an open mind all of this, boys. So, explain to me how this is supposed to work."

Shadow steps forward, mind-linking with us both, *'You haven't needed me for any spells or magic in a looong time. At most, I help you with control issues more than as a power reserve.'* He walks over to me and rests his head on my lap. *'You don't need me anymore. You know this.'*

I cup his big face in my hands, his fur so soft in my hands. Looking him in the eyes, "I'll always need you, but I understand. Do you understand what you are asking? I don't want to lose you Shadow, but I know I can't be selfish." Taking a deep breath and leaning my forehead against his big, furry head.

I know my powers and abilities have been growing for a while now; I knew it was just a matter of time before he asked to leave me. I just wasn't expecting it to hurt so much. The bonding spell that was performed when I was five was easy for me to cast under the direction of Maybelle; however, the separation spell will be trickier and painful for both of us, temporarily. It will feel like splitting the soul apart, as we have been together for so long.

"Are you sure this is what you want?" I ask Shadow again.

'I think this will be good for everyone. You don't need me, and the pack could use the help.' He looks up at me with his deep golden eyes.

Sighs...

'I never wanted to lose my best friend.' I mind-link with him solely.

'You'll never lose me. Especially, if you take over as pack Shaman.' He links back to me.

"This is a lot to think about over breakfast. I need to get ready for work. Let's table this for now and pick this back up later tonight." I tell them both as I get up and clear the table. I look over to Galen, "I'll see you at the hospital, right?"

He gets up from the table, walks over to me, leans down, and kisses my forehead. "You can count on that." He walks out the front door and leaves.

I stand there for a moment with Shadow.

It's quiet.

He's barely gone a mere few seconds and already I feel this ache in my chest.

The warmth that I felt when I was around him starts to fade.

What is this?

Shaking it off, I proceed with my shower and get ready for work.

Twelve

"**W**ELL, SOMEONE HAD A good weekend. Girl, you are just absolutely glowing." Brody winks over at me while eating lunch in our break room. It's the first chance we've had today to see each other. "Care to share any details with your friend?"

"It was a busy weekend," I replied blushing.

"That's it? That's all I get?"

I go back to eating my salad and playing on my phone, stress-relieving in any way I can while dealing with these crazy, sick patients. "What happened this weekend can't be discussed while at work or sober."

"So, does that mean we need to go out tonight and dance and drink our problems away?" He hints while flashing a big, sexy smile, showing off his perfectly white fangs.

"You could say that, but what problems could you possibly have? Last I knew, you didn't have any." I reply in between bites. Being a nurse, it's rare to find any time to eat, let alone to sit down and eat.

"You free to go out tonight? There is a new DJ at the Dark Illusion tonight; I've heard he's amazing."

Nodding my head, "should be fine to go out assuming nothing crazy happens between now and the end of shift."

Brody just snorts his laughter; this is Capital City, something crazy is always happening. We sit there in silence, enjoying each other's company and our meals. Just as I'm about to take another bite, I catch a faint whiff of pine heading toward our break room just as the door opens.

Galen is standing there in scrubs and a white doctor's coat, he looks directly at me and smiles. "Thought I might find you here. You mind if I borrow her Brody; we've got another victim in the ER that I need help with."

Brody and I break out into laughter, Galen's expression goes from happy to confused in an instant. Brody looks over at me, and winks, "Go get 'em, tiger. Give me your papers and I'll take over." He extends his hand out to take my report sheets.

I get up from the table and put away my salad, Galen still holding the door open for me, waiting for me; his dark predatory eyes watching me as I move. I dump my report sheets down in front of Brody and quickly kiss Brody's cheek, in a friend sort of way, "We'll catch up later tonight. I promise."

I walk through the door, barely squeezing by Galen's large frame. His pine scent invades my senses as I do. Our bodies slightly brush up against each other, causing us to look at each other for a brief moment. The chemistry between us freezing time for a split second, makes me forget that we are at work and that there is a patient who needs our help. I need to focus, but it's so hard to when he looks and smells like this.

Once in the hallway, the hustle and bustle of people going about their business bursts my bubble and snaps my attention to the problem at hand.

"So, who is the patient?" I ask him.

He hands me the tablet and starts to rattle off patient information and stats of what we know so far. I'm doing my best to listen to him and look at the patient's chart, but being this close to him, it's so hard to concentrate. Flipping through the patient's chart, it's very similar to that of Kelly. Both met up with friends and went out to Dark Illusion, had a few drinks, and a few hours later became aggressive, combative, and hysterical. I flip open Kelly's chart; both went to Dark Illusion and both patients are human.

I stop abruptly in the hallway, "Galen...uh, I mean Dr. Saunders, look at these two reports and tell me what you see." Handing him back the tablet and both patients' charts open to the same intake form.

He takes a few minutes to scan them over. "Dark Illusion? That can't be a coincidence."

I just stand there next to him, nodding in agreement, enjoying his pine scent. After we both arrive at the same conclusion, we resume walking back to the patient in the ER.

When we reached the patient's room, I expected to hear yelling.

I expected to hear a combative patient.

I expected to hear more than what we did.

I wasn't expecting the code team to be calling time-of-death on the patient.

The nurses start shutting off the machines; the insistent whine of the monitor showing no pulse is turned off first. The code team starts clearing out of the room and the nurses start clearing out the mess and writing down the facts.

Looking over at Galen, his face is an array of emotions: shock, anger, confusion, and he's pale. "What happened?!" He forgets himself for a moment as his Alpha aura explodes through the room, causing multiple shifters to stumble from his power. The air becomes hot and heavy to breathe, I take his hand in mine and grip it as hard as I can to bring his attention back to me. His hand is so hot, radiating as his aura throughout the room.

"Sedo," I manage to whisper, a white glow emits over our clasped hands, his aura starts shrinking, his power retreating back into himself. The air starts becoming easier to breathe once again.

Galen looks over at me, heat and desire burning from his eyes into mine. I let go of his hand, "Thank you," he whispers to me. I manage to nod my head slightly.

A nurse comes up to us, "I-I'm so sorry Dr. Saunders. After you went upstairs to get Nurse Spellcaster, the patient started coding. There was no time to get you back here."

"Thank you, Nurse Deirdre. You may go. All of you." He dismisses everyone.

Everyone starts to leave, all except Galen and myself. The room still has so much tension, despite being empty. I close my eyes and reach out with my magic, I can still feel so many emotions from the patient, it's like breadcrumbs to follow leading me back to his memories.

"Galen, I have an idea." I look at him, "I need you to get out."

He looks at me puzzled and just leaves, not questioning me or anything. I shut the door behind him and walk back towards the deceased patient on the bed.

Multiple bite marks and gashes are scattered all over the body. His face contorted with fear. Looking at his hands and fingers, I notice the same blue powder as with Kelly. I walk up to the head of the bed and place two fingers on each side of the patient's head, near the temporal area.

His body is still warm, this might just work...

Other medical professionals have been able to do this, but I have no idea how much power is needed, I just hope I have enough.

I reach out with my magic and focus on my goal. I've never tried to do this on anyone deceased; it's worth a shot, especially if it helps us with what is happening in our city.

A kaleidoscope of images, memories flashing through my head, each one unorganized and messy. I pull on my power from my reserves, sweat breaking out across my forehead from the strain. Images of people dancing and drinking, flashing lights, people all over each other in dark corners of the rooms, and people doing drugs, snorting a blue powder.

Dark Illusion; I recognize the room setup and decor any day.

I let go of the patient's mind as carefully as I can; the feeling of pulling out of someone else's mind is normally easier, but today it's like the connection snaps like a rubber band causing me to stumble back.

Woah...

Feeling drained, more than I expected, I go out of the room, fumbling with the door, and grab onto Galen's arm. He was talking to one of the other doctors from the code team. He immediately turns his attention to me, "You look like you've seen a ghost." He pulls me off to the side of the hallway and seats me down to the floor. "You look like death; you're shaky. What happened in there?"

"I've never done that before...I read a couple of different articles and studies where medical professionals who were supernatural had the ability to 'tap' into the minds of those recently deceased." feeling lightheaded and woozy, I close my eyes and focus on my breathing. "The articles just never said how much power you need to use, not like it's something you can really measure anyway. Every witch is different, every power source is different; so, I thought I would give it a try."

Galen squats down next to me, "Are you freaking kidding me?" placing a hand on my knee. "Are you sure you're ok?"

I manage to nod my head, leaning my head against the wall. "His mind was a mess, fragmented. It was like flashes of memory, not in any particular order, but it was familiar. Dark Illusion; same as Kelly, the last thing they both remembered was being with friends at Dark Illusion."

I look up at Galen, his expression dark and eyes filled with concern. "We need to talk with Forest.

I nod at him, "I'll call him and see if he can stop by the hospital-"

"No need," Galen interrupts me, "he's right over there. Looks like he's getting statements from the code team." He motions his fingers down the hallway.

Looking down the hallway, in the direction where Galen is pointing, Forest is standing there back slightly towards us, talking to a nurse and taking notes furiously. As if sensing us watching him, Forest turns and looks in our direction. He just nods to acknowledge us.

"Do you want to try to stand?" Galen asks.

I nod in agreement; he grips me up underneath my arm and back and pulls me up slowly with himself. "Thank you," I whisper, giving him a weak smile and straightening my scrubs. At least I'm no longer feeling like I'm going to have a syncopal episode, just drained beyond relief. Galen slides his hand down my arm and gently holds my hand, which is freezing from using so much magic; I welcome his warmth. Magic always has a price, and that was a lot of magic.

As Forest approaches us, I try to pull my hand away from Galen, but he holds on tighter. I look up at him, he shakes his head letting me know that he's not going to let go of me. His eyes glow for a moment, his Alpha self becoming territorial over me.

Oh, great...This is going to go over well, not...

Forest stops in front of us smiling, until he looks down to see Galen holding my hand, then his face changes. His eyes go dark and his face furrows; this isn't calm Forest who I have worked with, this Forest is upset that another man is staking claim over something that he wants. Forest may be a witch, but he's definitely Alpha in his own way.

"Nurse Spellcaster. Dr. Saunders." Forest says with a head nod, acknowledging us, being professional and cold.

"Forest," I say softly.

"Officer Monroe." Galen returns the greeting.

"Dr. Saunders, I heard this was your patient. Can you kindly tell me what happened and why Nurse Spellcaster is here and looks like she's seen a ghost?" He manages to ask Galen while reprimanding his professionalism at the same time.

"The patient was brought in, just like the one you and your partner brought in several days ago; completely combative and hysterical. We placed them in restraints for safety reasons." He answers Forest's questions while still holding onto my hand. "I left and went up to the unit to get Nurse Spellcaster here to see if she could assist with this case. When I left the patient was as stable as could be given the situation and when we came to the room, the code team was calling the time of death at 12:45."

"I see...I see..." Forest says as her scribbles something on his notepad

"Callie was able to 'tap' into the patient's mind briefly-" Galen starts to explain.

"Wait-you went in the room after the patient passed?!" Forest questions and looks at me angrily.

"I had read articles where supernatural healthcare professionals have been able to 'tap' into a patient's mind of the newly deceased-" I try to explain right before I'm interrupted again.

"Callie, do you realize that you could have tampered with evidence by performing that high level of magic?!" His demeanor changing from professional to not in an instant.

"I was very careful, Forest. You know me; I would never jeopardize a case or put my license at risk unnecessarily!" I shout at him. I can't believe how he's treating me. I've worked with him for years, he knows that I would never do anything without thinking things through.

"I'd like to ask you a few questions about what you 'did' and what you 'saw'...Alone." Forest looks Galen straight in the eyes with that last word.

Galen lets go of my hand but kisses the top of my head as Forest steps to the side to allow me to go forward. He leads me a few feet down the hall, with his hand on the small of my back.

"So, you and Galen now? How long has that been going on?" Forest starts questioning me; feeling slightly attacked by his questions that are way off base and not relevant to why he's here.

"That's none of your business Forest!" I respond quickly to him. "That has nothing to do with the case and YOU know it." Reminding him to get back to the task at hand. I don't particularly like being attacked about who is involved in my life, and I make it known by folding my arms over my chest and leaning against the wall, waiting for questions that are related to this case.

"You're right, I'm sorry." He clears his throat, adjusts the collar of his uniform, and flips open to a blank page in his notepad, "so, Callie, can you tell me what happened after the patient died? I need to know in detail what you did and what you saw."

And so, I did.

I explained to Forest about the scientific medical journals that had published articles about supernatural healthcare providers using magic on the nearly deceased. I explained to him my technique and my best efforts to not contaminate the patient or the exam room. I explained in as much detail as I could about the patient's memories.

Forest also made me go on the record that I have never performed this type of magic on a deceased patient before and did so without any supervision. Slightly irritated that he made me do this, but he's a professional as well and has a job to do.

I did remind him and have him add that I have performed this type of magic on living patients and shared memories with others before successfully; whether he actually acknowledged it or not, I have no idea.

I don't know how long we stood in the hallway talking, or rather him interrogating me with endless questions. His questions make me feel like I'm being attacked like I'm the reason the patient is dead or something. This man in front of me is so cold, so different than the man I had an intimate evening with just the other night.

I keep reminding myself that he's here to do his job. He's being professional. He's not smiling though. There's no playfulness in his mannerisms. There's no flirting. I reach out with my magic, the little that I have left, and hit a wall. He keeps asking me questions and writing down my answers as if he doesn't feel me trying to read him. I just kept answering his questions, pretending that I didn't just try to read him either.

He's never blocked me out before...

Galen walks up beside me and places a hand on my shoulder, maintaining eye contact with Forest, like he's the enemy or something. His hand on my shoulder is warm and heavy, reminding me that I'm not going through this alone.

"Brody is calling for her back upstairs. You get everything?" Galen asks as professionally as possible.

"Yeah, I think I have everything." He closes his notepad and looks at me, "I'll call you if I need anything else." He nods to both of us and then walks away.

He doesn't say bye.

Or say that he'll call me later.

Or smile.

He just turns and walks away, like I don't even matter.

Like we didn't just have an amazing date, even if it did get interrupted.

"What was that about?" Galen asks me while I watch Forest walk away.

I just shrug my shoulders, needing to shake off the butt-hurt feelings that Forest left behind. I start to make my way back up to my unit when Galen reaches for my hand and stops me.

"Don't be mad at Forest. He saw you with me and drew up his own conclusions. Can't blame the guy for being hurt." Galen's voice slides over me like melted chocolate, dark and seductive.

"You helped him make those *premature* decisions."

"Premature? Still trying to resist your fate?" He goads.

"I haven't decided yet. And this display of macho territorial Alpha shit needs to stop, or you'll make the decision for me." I throw back at him, ripping my hand out of his grip, and make my way back upstairs to finish my shift.

I need to get out tonight...

I need a drink...

Thirteen

I CLOSE MY EYES, lean against Brody, and just let the music carry us away. The club's enchanting atmosphere surrounds us as we walk through the crowd, creating a palpable sense of anticipation. I wrap my hands up around Brody's neck as we continue to dance, making our way through the crowd. Brody's hands start moving possessively across my stomach, keeping me flat against him, his erection pressed firmly against my ass.

Dark Illusion offers us the perfect opportunity to take a break from our professional lives, all while alluring us with seductive music and many dark corners. The music resonates through my body as Brody and I make our way through the crowds; our bodies weave through the crowd, the bass pulsating throughout my whole body, allowing our bodies to sync up to the captivating beat. As we dance, I lose myself in the music's rhythm and the liberating sensation of being alive, free from hospital concerns, as my body presses against Brody's.

My dress is short and black, a killer combination of mystery and sexuality, drawing attention as we make our way through the dark passages to the dance floor. Brody brings attention to himself as well; wearing fitted jeans and a white tee shirt reflecting the club's lights. Wearing my audacious attire, we exude a certain magnetism that causes people to gaze and whisper in our direction, treating us like celebrities. As we approach the center of the club, a wave of joy rushes through me, intensified by the vibrant lights and music enveloping us. With Brody by my side, we dive into the crowd and embrace the extravagant ambiance of Dark Illusion.

"I'm glad you came out with me tonight. I've missed this." Brody confesses into my ear. I give his neck a tight squeeze in response and smile up at him, both of us still dancing to the beat. He flashes me his gorgeous smile with a little fang popping out.

Right there, amidst the flashing lights and pounding music, we end up somewhat intertwined in a dance that is more than just movement. Moving in unison, our bodies form a familiar dance, each step quietly acknowledging our tantalizing connection. Brody's touch moves over my body and kindles a blaze deep inside me, a glow that finds its way into the very center of my core.

As Brody and I move together, his hands igniting the fire in me, I gaze upon jealous onlookers.

They all want Brody...

The way we dance feels almost too intimate, wishing there could be more between us; a special secret that I've never shared with anyone, not even Shadow. I notice a large, shadowy figure at the bar. A shadowy figure with a pair of golden eyes, staring at us from the bar. Golden-eyes that go with a body that's completely jacked from what I can tell from halfway across the room. I was about to tell Brody that we are being watched, but by the time I look back at the bar, Golden-eyes has vanished.

Great, now I'm hallucinating...

I shrug it off and continue dancing up against Brody, feeling safe in his arms and enjoying the night off. I don't think any more of it until another body starts dancing up against the front of me, sandwiching me between this body and Brody; almost any girl's fantasy. I look up and lock eyes with the Golden-eyes, from across the room just a moment ago, dancing up against me.

Just as Golden-eyes goes to move his hands to my hips, Brody intervenes, smacking his hands away forcefully and pushing me behind him, taking a protective stance. Fangs bared towards Golden-eyes, and Brody maintains one hand to keep me behind him.

"Jesus, Brody! It's me, Declan." Golden-eyes shouts over the music.

Declan.... that name is familiar.

As realization hits Brody, he relaxes as he comes out of the haze of our dancing and retracts his fangs. "Declan? What are you doing here?" He demands, still standing in front of me, keeping contact with me. I grip onto his bicep with one hand and hold my other hand out, palm out facing Golden-eyes readying myself to spell-cast for protection.

Declan leans forward, close into Brody, sniffing him and towards me. "Damn, she smells good." *Sniff, sniff.* "Witch for sure, but there is something else there.... Hmmm, you haven't claimed her yet Brody?" Declan's voice is deep and smooth, like what you would expect from someone who is like Brody, a vampire.

Brody hisses and bares his fangs towards Declan once more. "Back off Declan. She's mine!" He declares loudly enough for surrounding onlookers to hear.

Claimed her? What the hell is going on? Brody's gay, why would he claim me?

This is ridiculous, not that I'm afraid of Golden-eyes here, but the way Brody is acting makes me feel like I shouldn't correct him or leave his side right now. My grip on his arm tightens, not out of fear, but out of the unknown of what is going on between these two.

"Easy man, I'm not going to even try to compete. It's obvious by the way she was dancing with you and how she clings to you, that she's yours." Golden-eyes raises his hands up in surrender.

"What do you want?" Brody asks again.

"Can we talk somewhere more private?" Golden-eyes leans forward and whispers into Brody's ear. The music is too loud for me to hear anything.

Brody turns towards me, allowing me to see the full figure of Declan. "Callie, allow me to introduce you to Declan. He's the Second to the Queen." Brody introduces as Declan nods his head towards me.

The Queen.

The Vampire Queen.

Ooohh...

I hold out my hand to shake his hand, however Declan clasps my hand and turns it over to kiss my knuckles. Getting a shiver of anxiety, I peel my hand away out from his grasp. Declan looks at Brody again, reading between the lines of their body language, I excuse myself as politely as I possibly can "I'm going to the bar. I need a drink and a snack." I smile at Brody before making my way towards the bar.

It doesn't take long for them to start arguing, hands moving as they talk, I head towards the bar where Dizzy is in the center of the action. She is Dark Illusion's best bartender, who is also a rogue werewolf. Dizzy is probably one of my closest friends and has been since I moved to the city after leaving the pack.

"Hi, Dizzy!" I greeted with a smile, the tension from earlier melting away at the sight of my favorite bartender. Standing at 5'5", very fit and toned, her tanned skin covered in tattoos and hair pulled back in multiple braids. Despite the overwhelming stress and anxiety I'm experiencing, being by Dizzy's side brings me profound relaxation, as her demeanor acts as a cure for my anxiousness and exhaustion.

Leaning nonchalantly against the bar, Dizzy chuckles with mischief sparkling in her eyes. "Look who decided to join us, the beautiful Callie Spellcaster. Are we sticking to the usual tonight?"

With gratitude, I nod and find solace in the familiar banter. "Dizzy, you have an uncanny ability to know me too well. Can I have an extra fruity Blue Sex Sling, please?" Watching Dizzy effortlessly prepare my drink, I decide it's the perfect moment to address something that has been weighing on me. "Dizzy, have you heard any scandalous gossip at the club recently?"

Pausing with a hint of secrecy, Dizzy scans the room before leaning in. "There's always a lot of rumors going around about the club. Recently, there have been rumors of some suspicious activities happening."

With my curiosity peaked, I lean closer to Dizzy, practically lying on top of the bar counter.

Dizzy leans forward, whispering into my ear, "I wouldn't worry too much over it though. Max will get to the bottom of it and take care of things...his way. I almost feel sorry for the idiot who thinks that they can get away with such dealings, Max is furious. I wouldn't want to be on the other end of all this."

My mind fills with thoughts of the possible implications, "Does Max have any idea concerning who might be responsible?"

Dizzy just shrugs and goes back to her work.

As I process the information, a feeling of unease begins to take hold in my mind; Dizzy places my drink in front of me on the bar top. "Thanks for letting me know, Diz. You're my hero." This drink is just what I need.

"Anytime, Callie," Dizzy says, winking and smiling warmly.

I spin around on my stool, seeing Brody and Declan still arguing, hand gestures flying through the air. I turn back around, "Hey Dizzy, any chance you can hear what they are going on about?"

Dizzy looks over my shoulder over at Brody and Declan, tucking a few braids behind her ear, chuckling slightly. "I would let you in, but I think it's more of a lover's quarrel than anything. And something about Brody being summoned back to the Nest..."

The Nest...

I can feel all the blood drain from my face. The Nest is the Home of the Vampire Queen. I never hear Brody talk about his family or reference the Queen at all, so I'm not really sure where his allegiance lies, but to disregard a formal summons and having Declan appear only adds to my already rising anxiety from his presence.

With my cocktail in hand, I slide off my stool and make my way back towards Brody and the dance floor, hoping to salvage the night and smooth over his temper. Savoring the familiar sweetness of the drink, I can't shake the small feeling that something bad might happen tonight. Every sip I take of the Blue Sex Sling, I can sense its potent blend enchanting me. Initially, my taste buds were delighted by a burst of fruity flavor, and then a soothing warmth enveloped me, causing my muscles and inhibitions to unwind.

As I drink and dance my way back to Brody, the bass of the music flows through my body. Brody turns towards me and smiles, watching me dance with my drink in my hand. I see him lean towards Declan and whisper something in his ear, Declan nods and leaves. Whatever Brody said seemed to work; *good*!

I lose my footing for just a moment, head spinning slightly, Brody sweeps right in grabbing me around the waist and pulling me hard up against him, my hand landing in the middle of his chest while the other maintains to hold on to my drink. Chuckling, he whispers into my ear, "How many drinks did you have?"

"Just the one, I swear."

The combination of that drink and the noise in the club makes it hard for me to stay composed; I can feel my mind spiraling as my mind races and feels overwhelmed. Fear and anxiety start creeping in the back of my mind. My mind fraying, making it harder to maintain control. There is doubt creeping under my alcohol-dreamy façade. I'm scared as I attempt to connect with Shadow using my magic, hoping to summon my usual power, but instead, I feel an unsettling void that leaves me cold, feeble, and bewildered.

What was in that drink?

I know I haven't been out in a long time, but this drink is hitting harder than what it should. Without my magic to protect me, I am truly vulnerable to the dangers of Dark Illusion, and my mind is dulled by a strong cocktail.

"Brody... I think I need to call it a night." I whisper to him. Seeing the fear in my eyes, Brody nods and starts to lead us to the door. As I stumble along behind him, my mind cloudy with doubt and my body feeling weak, I can't shake the feeling that we are in more danger at this moment than I could have imagined.

As Brody and I enter the cold night air, leaving the pounding heart of Dark Illusion, the remnants of the city's vibrant energy still hang around us. Brody takes my hand as we walk back to my parked Jeep on the street.

"Callie," Brody's soft voice barely registers in my head as I stumble and try to catch my footing, "we need to talk."

I shift my gaze to him, my mind still intoxicated by the powerful cocktail. The world feels like it is disappearing while I focus intently on Brody's words, my thoughts are muddled and a foggy feeling overcomes me, making everything seem to move in slow motion.

He holds my hand firmly in his, halting in his steps, causing me to collide with him. He places his hands on my shoulders, to keep me from falling over. Brody hesitates, his voice and face matching how nervous he is as he confesses more, his words spinning around my head, "Callie, I have feelings for you beyond friendship. No matter how hard I try to deny it, my feelings are impossible to ignore."

Brody's confession weighs heavily in the air as my heart races, making it difficult to comprehend the impact of his words due to the lingering effects of the drink.

"A-and you should know that I'm aware of Galen," Brody's confession continues, his eyes scanning for my reaction, "I know you and he have something extraordinary, something I can never match. Despite my reservations, I'm willing to share you with him, Callie."

I can't mistake the sincerity in Brody's voice; his words were incredibly honest and leave me in awe. Amidst conflicting emotions, duties, and feeling drunk off my ass, I find it hard to come to terms with Brody's revelation. The concept of being in an open relationship with Galen and Brody is simultaneously exhilarating and scary. Guilt arises as I experience conflicting emotions. In the midst of my troubled mind, I realize that it might be worth exploring the connections and emotions we share.

As Brody and I approach my Jeep, my world is spinning, the effects of that drink clearly hit me harder and longer than before. Brody holds on to my hand as if waiting for my return confession. I'm vocally paralyzed by the fact that both Galen and Brody want me and that Brody is willing to share his affection for me with Galen. That's such a vampire thing.

Next time, I need to tell Diz to not make it so strong, I'm thinking crazy thoughts.

Before we take another step, I feel a sharp sting on the left side of my neck. I reach up to my neck and pull back with a syringe in my hand, the plunger pressed in and the contents injected into my neck.

A tranquilizer?

From behind, a group of masked assailants emerged and encircled us. With precision and speed, they move closer to us. A strong arm wraps around my waist, pinning my arms down by my sides, separating me from Brody. My struggles seem futile as a deep voice chuckles at my weakened state. In the final moments, before everything goes dark, I catch a glimpse of Brody being attacked by several masked assailants, fighting back fearlessly. The very last thing I see, before passing out, is Brody going down and the sound of Brody's voice, a bone-chilling scream fading into the darkness of night.

Fourteen

C OLD...
		Darkness...
Pitch black...
Pain...
My head...
Why am I cold?
Why do my arms and legs feel so heavy?
Where am I?
My eyes flutter open, revealing that I'm lying on concrete flooring in a single candle-lit room. I attempt to move, but my arms and legs cry out in pain as rope bites into my skin. I look around and can barely make out my surroundings, the room is small, dirty, and empty of life except for me. There is more light coming from underneath the door, which looks to be the only way in or out of this room. The air is thick with moisture as if breathing through a soggy cloth; suffocating with the smell of damp earth, rot, and metal.

Blood?

Death?

The sound of distant footsteps echoed through the darkness, sending shivers down my spine.

"Brody?!" I whisper, attempting to find my friend without alerting whoever that I'm awake. I wait a few moments, hoping to hear Brody's voice, however, there is no answer. Only silence answers my call, no sign of my friend in the darkness.

I feel a sense of dread as the reality sinks in, and my mind starts racing with endless possibilities. I attempt to reach within myself to where my magic lies and hit a wall of pain. Excruciating pain causes my vision to blur and fade to black.

Fear wraps around me tightly, chilling my body to my core. My heart is pounding so fast that I can barely catch my breath. My body trembles, every nerve tense, envisioning the worst lurking in the dark. The unknown is similar to a lurking creature, poised to swallow me whole.

Unable to move, I lay my head back down on the ground, closing my eyes. Hoping that this is just a nightmare, hoping that I wake up in my warm bed. Footsteps echo again in the darkness on the other side of the door, voices muffled by the door, but unable to make out what is said. I attempt to reach out to my magic again, instant agonizing pain slices through my body, causing my vision to blur. The pain vibrates so severely throughout my body, unable to take the pain, my strength gives out and I lose consciousness once again.

***

"You must wake Calista. It's not your time yet..."

A feminine voice awakens me suddenly, startling me so that the rope that binds me bites into my flesh more. I grind my teeth and groan against my bindings.

BANG!

Light floods through the room as the door forcefully swings open. I try to squirm back, hitting the wall behind me. A tall figure comes in, dressed in black, wearing the same white mask that kidnapped and did who knows what to Brody. The figure crouches down in front of me, bringing their hand up to grip my chin, forcing me to look at them. All I see are a pair of eyes, gray-blue eyes, strikingly brilliant.

"If you want to live, you'll do as you're told." The masked figure's voice is deep and muffled, and definitely masculine. The grip on my chin makes me painfully aware that I am defenseless.

"Wh-what do you want with me? Where's Brody? Where am I?" I spit out without even thinking.

The masked man chuckles deeply, "You're about to find out." He stands up and grabs my ropes, pulling me up and throwing me over his shoulder. I try to kick and throw my weight into him to put me down, I know that this isn't going to go in my favor if I leave this room. He drops me back to the ground, leans over me, and grabs my throat. "Knock it off. I'm not allowed to hurt you. Not yet anyway, but don't tempt me to disobey my orders"

I struggle to breathe from under his grip. He releases my throat and picks me back up, throwing me back over his shoulder. Walking out of the room and going down the hallway, I notice debris littering the sides of the hallway. Lights flickering on and off the ceiling. Medical equipment haphazardly lying around. The tiles are broken on the sides of the walls and missing on the floor. Blood and dirt smeared together. Realization hits, and I know where I am.

The old hospital in the Warehouse district...

No... This can't be...

I won't break.

Beneath the surface, a blazing fire ignites, fueling an unwavering determination to persevere. They will not succeed under any circumstances. I will do whatever it takes, fighting fiercely and fearlessly, to overcome anything that they throw at me.

My kidnapper takes many twists and turns down different hallways and staircases. Each hallway looking just the same, causing me to lose track of where we are within the building. It's not until my kidnapper bursts through a set of huge double doors, stopping in the center of a large room that my head stops spinning from moving. He slides me off his shoulders, like a sack of potatoes, causing me to land hard on my ass.

THUMP!

"Dude, what the…" I look up at my kidnapper and am about to give him a piece of my mind for dropping me on the floor.

"Quiet!" He shouts down to me. He takes a few steps forward, leaving me on the floor behind him. I take a moment to look around the room, my gaze following my kidnapper's movements.

At the far end of the room is a dias with a throne-like chair upon it. Sitting on that chair is a beautiful, pale woman. The first thing I notice is her eyes, brilliant ice blue. Her skin is so pale that it makes her eyes sparkle that much more. Her hair is trussed up into a messy bun with a few strains of hair outlining her face, and a simple tiara nestled elegantly in her hair. Her beauty is nothing I've ever seen before, eerie with a side of deadly.

The woman stands up from her seat and starts to make her way down the steps to greet my kidnapper, who instantly kneels to the floor and bows his head. He maintains this composure until the woman is standing directly in front of me, holding her hand out to him.

He takes her hand in his and kisses her knuckles. "My Queen."

Queen??

As in the Vampire Queen??

Oh shit…

"What did you bring me my love?" She asks, her voice calm and soft as if hiding her deadliness.

"This is the witch that you asked for." He rises and answers plainly, paying me no mind, giving all his attention to the woman in front of him.

Her face instantly changes as the realization of who I am sinks in. She walks towards me, bends down, and grabs my chin with her pale, cold fingers, her nails digging into my flesh like a knife slicing through butter. Bruising my chin with practically no effort at all.

"Look at me." She demands, her voice stern and dominant.

With no choice but to comply, I glance up at her. Her deep gaze pierces me with her icy blue eyes. Those eyes slash through me like daggers aimed at carving out my soul. Her gaze is so intense that it gives me the chills. I can feel myself getting lost in her eyes and suddenly she gasps, drops my chin abruptly, and backs away. She turns her back to me and starts to walk back towards her Dias.

"Wh-who are you?" I ask, trying to mask my panic and fear with courage.

She turns around on the steps. "Who am I? Who am I?" She laughs, which sounds like a siren's song, seductive and danger-ous. "My dear, I'm the Queen. Of the Vampires." She returns to her throne and gracefully sits tall.

With my kidnapper pulling me towards the Dias, the Queen's presence engulfs me like stepping into the eye of a storm. She possesses a commanding presence on her throne that emanates power and authority. I can feel its heaviness, making me shrink down even more to the floor. My kidnapper returns to my side, grabbing the ropes that bind me so, and yanking me towards the Dias.

"Why am I here? What do you want from me?" I struggle to maintain my composure and strength while being bound, trying my best to not move too much to prevent the rope's bite from continuing to dig into my skin.

She looks down at me, silence is deafening.

A moment passes before she raises her as if summoning another. Behind her throne, Declan comes up to her left side, standing in full view of me. He leans forward for her to whisper in his ear, she grabs onto his arm possessively, and stares down at us, giving away that she is talking about us. I can feel my kidnapper tense up, becoming uneasy at the sight of Declan, almost possessively.

Is there some sort of power struggle between them?

She called my kidnapper my love, but the way she holds onto Declan's arm is suggestive of sexual tension as well. Oh, it's crystal clear, the Queen holds all the cards in this deadly game, and I want nothing to do with any of this. With a head nod, Declan leaves the Dias, walking down the steps, past me, and leaves the room. The Queen just sits there on her throne, smiling down at me. Minutes go by and the silence is deafening, it's as if time is frozen in place.

I need to figure out how to get out of here...

What is she waiting for?

I remain silent, knowing full well that she could kill me in an instant and not think twice about it. I need to be smart about this, especially since I don't have access to my magic. No thanks to whatever is in that syringe my kidnapper keeps injecting me with. I know deep down I'm at her mercy. Her silent threat and her power hangs in the air like a storm cloud, a constant reminder of what could happen if I step out of line.

The door behind us creeks back open. I turn my attention and see Declan returning with two more men. It's not until Declan comes closer to us that I see that the two men, trailing behind Declan, are dragging a figure underneath the arms. When the two men get to the bottom of the stairs of Dias, they drop the body on the floor.

Upon closer examination, I see the figure that was dropped heavily to the floor is Brody. He's been beaten up, more like tortured, into a bloody pulp. He's breathing, but one eye is swollen shut and he has multiple stab wounds littered all over. I try to scoot closer to him, I can't help but feel that this is all my fault.

If Brody and I hadn't been out, none of this would have happened...

"Brody?" I whisper to him. My kidnapper reaches forward and places one of his hands on my shoulder, preventing me from getting any closer to Brody.

"So, I believe you know my brother." The Queen says leaning forward, smiling like the Cheshire Cat, showing off her fangs.

"Your brother?" No, it can't be. "Brody is your brother?" At first, I'm in shock. There is no way that Brody is the brother to the Queen. He would have told me, wouldn't he?

"Not just my brother dear. He's my twin." The Queen drops a bomb. She rambles on more about how Brody could have been King if he hadn't stepped down to become a nurse. She mocks him for wanting to help for the sick and injured. She continues about how he yearned to keep hold of his humanity, and how doing so has made him weak.

"Elona...please?" A weak plea escapes from Brody.

"Oh, hello my dear, pathetic brother. Have you had enough fun with Declan already? Are you ready to take your rightful place within the Nest?" She's goading him. Brody will never give up his humanity, not to join this psychotic bitch.

Behind Elona's, I find Declan standing there with such a powerful stare; there's a hunger in his eyes, a hunger for more of Brody, well Brody's torture anyway... In his own way, he is a force to be reckoned with, devoted to the queen but with a ruthless streak. His eyes reveal a simmering tension. He remains loyal to his Queen, but what will he sacrifice?

How could Declan do that to Brody?

Brody can't even get up off the floor he's been beaten down so much. He's so weak, watching him laying there on the floor; he just lays there shaking his head no over and over. I would do anything to stop it. As if sensing my thoughts, the Queen looks up at me.

"Something you want to say, Calista?" The Queen's voice is cold and daring me to speak up.

"What do you want with us? Haven't you done enough to him?" My voice shaking, and all my confidence has shattered seeing what they are capable of doing to one of their own. I don't stand a chance without my magic.

"I have only just begun. My lover asked for you specifically, especially when we found out that Brody here has feelings for you. I'm inclined to let him play with you. To prove a point." She states with hate and anger towards Brody and myself.

A point?

What point could she possibly be trying to make?

It's at this moment, that the Queen reveals her involvement in the drug problem in Capital City, admitting she has a team of scientists and pharmacists working on experimental synthetic drugs. The influx of information feels overwhelming, like a punch in the stomach. Her faith in her subjects and those loyal to her is unnerving, actually believing she will get away with it in the end. I already had my suspicions about her shady behavior, but this takes it to another level. She speaks of it as though it were a clandestine, cutting-edge operation meant to keep hidden from prying eyes.

She's completely off her rocker!

She persists in boasting about her entire operation. Preening and gloating, the Vampire Queen brags about her extensive body count of humans and supernatural creatures. She talks about the dishonest and crooked cops in Capital City. It's a clear indication of how deeply she has control over this city.

Are the city officials really this corrupt?

Why are they deliberately turning a blind eye?

What does she have on all of them?

It's like I'm living in a nightmare. The trustworthiness of those entrusted with your protection is called into question when they join forces with the enemy.

There's no question that the city is in trouble. The presence of this synthetic drug on the streets is like a ticking time bomb. With this synthetic drug flooding the streets, it's only a matter of time before this drug spreads to neighboring cities and becomes the next big hit, like meth or heroin.

I must find a solution to this chaos and bring the truth to light before it becomes untamable.

"Now, that you have heard everything. I'm going to give you a choice Calista. Join me? Or don't and my lover gets to have his way with you, however he likes." She stares down at us, waiting for my answer.

Not much of a choice.

She's lost her god-damn mind if she thinks I'm joining her and her circus.

"No. Never." My answer only causes her to smile. She waves her hands at me, dismissing me, allowing my kidnapper to pick me back up and throw me back over his shoulder. I kick and scream, not making it easy to be hauled away.

"CALLIE!" I look up to see Brody attempting to crawl to me; unable to stand, dragging himself, the lower half of his body completely limp as he attempts to get to me.

"BRODY!" I scream back to him, struggling and wiggling as much as I can within the grasp of my kidnapper. Which is as useless as ever.

With the trick of vampire speed, Declan is standing in front of Brody, swinging his fist and knocking Brody back down to the floor. More vampires appear out of nowhere and start to form a circle around Declan and Brody, there are just too many vampires. My heart pains as I know they are going to do whatever it takes to break him.

And me.

My kidnapper doesn't stop walking away or hesitate at the sounds of violence that ensues behind us. He walks, with me over his shoulder once more, through the double doors and continues back down the hallways. The doors shut loudly, silencing all sounds within the room and blocking my view of the beating Brody is receiving. I continue to struggle against my kidnapper.

They won't break me.

I can't let them break me.

Fifteen

T HE QUEEN'S OFFER TO join her seemed absolutely ridiculous until now.

My kidnapper now has complete power over me.

Despite the odds against me, I won't retreat. I can't retreat. What is it that the Borg says, 'resistance is futile'? But I must resist, I must do whatever I can to stay alive, at all costs.

No matter how many tempting offers the Queen dangles, I won't give in.

My kidnapper continues to take many twists and turns, all the hallways and doors look the same; dirty and broken equipment littered everywhere. I've lost track of where we are, not that it matters. No one will be able to find me here, no one knows where I am.

Shadow.

He knew I was going out. He'll get worried and come for me, but to what end? There are too many vampires here for him to take on alone. My heart saddens at the thought that I'll never see him again.

I can't even remember what we last spoke about...

The war fighting inside my head is useless. Fear and panic are playing a tennis match, while deep down I need to keep my strength hidden from my kidnapper. I have to get out of here. I will get out of here. I won't break, they won't win. My magic will return, I know it will, once these drugs are out of my system.

My kidnapper stops suddenly. I look up over his shoulder, he's stopped in front of a door, halfway down some random hallway. He doesn't move, except to turn his masked face to me.

"Last chance. Are you sure you don't want to take the Queen up on her offer? Because once we go through the door, game over for you" His voice is deep and stern. If he wasn't my kidnapper, it's the type of voice that you fantasize about.

Without even thinking, I say the first thing that comes to mind, "You all can go to hell" and regret it instantly. My kidnapper just chuckles as he busts open the door and flicks on the light switch.

The room appears to be an old exam room.

A lamp on the counter gives off a soft glow, illuminating the room just enough to make out furniture and multiple medical machines that are used for who knows what; there is a drager monitor and IV bump with fluids ready to go. This room is cleaner than the hallway. Everything is organized and placed in a strategic order.

My kidnapper must use this room for his own personal space as well; off in the corner is a bed that has been neatly made, a desk with a laptop, and multiple computer monitors showing the security cameras set up for the building. What catches my eye is that in the center of the room is a gurney. A gurney with restraints in place, the metal clasps glinting in the dim light. It's almost as if my kidnapper knew this was going to happen.

My kidnapper walks to the gurney and throws me down. His speed at which he restrains me down makes me wonder if he's a vampire too or if I'm just so drugged that I'm too slow for my own good. I test the restraints, which prove that I'm not going anywhere.

There is a smell, different from where I was previously. It lingers, invading my senses, a metallic tang of blood mixing with a sharp scent of herbs. The smell causes the room to spin and make me feel queasy,

My kidnapper is a witch?

Why would a witch work with vampires? Let alone this psychotic bitch of a Queen.

A sharp sting is felt in my restrained arm. I look and see my kidnapper is injecting me with more of that vile blue liquid. I grimace from the sensation as I feel the blue liquid crawling up my arm and burning throughout my body. The kidnapper disposes of the empty syringe and turns back toward me. His eyes are hungry.

SMACK!

Pain rips through my face as my kidnapper's blow landed on my left cheek. I feel the heat instantly erupt on my skin and tears welt from my eyes, forcing me to close them. I feel a cool breeze upon my body as the fabric is ripped away from my body. Opening my eyes to see the glint of a knife trailing down my dress, shredding the fabric in the process, revealing me down to just my black lace bra and matching panties. Goosebumps spring to life over my body as my kidnapper rips away the remains of my dress, forcing my nipples to push against the lace fabric of my bra.

He brushes the back of his knuckles against my skin, starting against the top of my thigh and trailing up slowly until he reaches my left breast. Through my bra, he forcefully grabs my breast whole with his massive hands. I grimace again at the pain, and I struggle against my restraints.

I lock eyes with him, "Take off your mask! Let me see who you are."

He chuckles at my demand.

"All in due time, princess."

My vision starts to blur as the drug takes effect.

My last fleeting thought before my world turns black, is that Shadow will have to find himself a new witch to train, how I have failed to listen to him...

Stop thinking like that, this is far from over.

***

Drip...drip...drip...

All I can hear is the drip, drip, drip of water somewhere in the darkness. It's like a clock ticking away the seconds, reminding me that time is passing, whether I like it or not. This room, it's like a pit of despair, forgotten by the world outside. It's where hope comes to die, where you're left to rot with no chance of escape. And the silence... it's so loud, it feels like it's crushing me.

Feeling like I'm caught in continuous brain fog, it takes me a moment to register that I'm cold. I look down and see that I no longer have my bra or panties on, they lay in shreds on the floor by the desk. There are various bruises starting to form all over my body.

How long have I been here?

What day is it?

All I need now is for my crazy kidnapper to appear...

The door opens and walks in the devil himself, still wearing the ski mask and white face mask over it. "Good morning princess. Are you ready to play?"

"It seems you started without me." Looking down at my body, seeing my clothes ripped and torn to tatters. "H-how long have I been out?"

"Three days."

Three days?

No, it's not possible...

He just chuckles and walks over to his desk, while I digest the information. With his back facing me, blocking my view from what he is planning to do next, all I can hear is him moving things around, the occasional clink of metal and glass. He turns around to face me, holding another syringe in his hand.

"No, please! I'll behave, just don't knock me out again." I beg. I thought that I would never beg, but at this point, I'll do anything to not black out again. I can't lose out on three days again. I thrash against my restraints as if I have any control or power in this situation.

"Oh princess, you're mistaken. This isn't meant to make you pass out, just to tamper with your magic so that you can't use it. I wouldn't want you calling your beast of a familiar to the rescue and ruining all my fun now." He smirks as he grips my arm and injects the drug into me. I hiss from the sting of my needle and feel the medication enter my bloodstream. My head starts swimming as I feel the medication taking over, and my body starts to get hot; whatever this drug is, it works fast.

He leans forward, whispering into my ear, "Let's see what we can do to keep you awake though. I prefer my toys to be conscious and...screaming." He runs his fingertips over my skin lightly around my navel, my body reacting to his touch in ways I wish it wouldn't. I try to squirm away from his touch, but it's useless, my restraints tighten as I try to move away from him. He grins seeing my body respond to him. His touch feels like hot rocks on my skin, rough and heating me up all at the same time.

He backs a couple of steps away from me, just looking at me. His eyes are filled with a hunger that frightens me. He walks around the gurney and presses a button; a bright light clicks on above me, so blinding bright that it forces me to shut my eyes, the bright light only adds to the disorientation feeling from the drugs. I hear my kidnapper walk back in front of me, my restraints start to feel loose, but my limbs are too heavy for me to take advantage and make a run for it.

If only I had access to my magic, this guy would be flattened in a heartbeat. Just as my kidnapper loosens my ankle restraints, he lifts me up over his shoulder again.

SLAP!

The hot sting on my ass jolts my body and mind back, but not completely enough to allow me any strength to fight off this psycho. He walks across the room, with just a few strides, and slides me down to my feet, facing a cold concrete wall. Before I can object or say anything, my kidnapper restrains my arms above me, with shackles hanging from the ceiling, as fast as he was able to restrain me to the gurney in the first place.

As he clips the last restraint in place, he stands with his body flushed with my backside. I can feel that all of this is arousing to him as his erection is pressed firmly up against me. He slowly trails his fingers down my arms, across my shoulders, making his way down my back, taking his time as he enjoys making goosebumps spring to life over my skin. He brings a hand up and grabs a fist full of my hair, pulling back, causing me to arch my neck and back simultaneously.

"Your skin is so beautiful and unmarked. We're going to fix that princess and you're going to love every minute of it!" His voice reeling with excitement, his hot breath on my skin, smelling heavily of coffee, adds to my anxiety. He pulls my hair back more causing me to arch more and forcing me up on my tiptoes. "You're mine Callie, don't ever forget that." He lets go of my hair, pushing me forward so that my face slams into the wall.

A wave of vertigo occurs immediately after my head hits the wall. My world spins as the pain ricochets through my head deafening, my ears ring out from the pain. As I struggle to get my bearings, I can feel dirt and grime from the wall sticking to my face. My vision blurs from meeting the wall that it takes a few moments before it clears as best as it can.

My kidnapper moves my legs farther apart and I feel him restrain them and hear the clicks on metal. I look down at my ankles to see a spreader bar is now in place, forcing me to keep my legs spread, allowing my kidnapper full access to not just my backside, but also my sex. A few moments pass between us, total silence, I can feel his gaze on my backside.

Pushing the buttons of my kidnapper, I open my mouth before I even think, "Are you just going to stand there all day? Take a picture, it's lasts longer—"

SLAP!

Pain, excruciating pain rips across my back. Unlike any pain that I've felt before; and different than the slap on my ass or the pain from getting my head thrown into the wall. My vision instantly blurs from the tears in my eyes, the pain turns to a sting as I feel moisture slide down my back.

"Did you like that princess? I've got plenty more where that came from." He laughs and starts pacing the room while I regain my composure. I turn my head to see my kidnapper holding what looks to be like a whip. A single-tail whip with a metal tip, a single drop of blood falls to the floor.

What the hell...

The sting increases as my kidnapper steps closer enough to blow air across my back. "Your back looks so beautiful, pink with red flowing down your pale skin." He brings his fingertips up to my back, my whole body tenses up as his fingers run along the new wound. He brings his fingertips to my face, showing me my own blood coating against his skin. He then brings his fingertip up to his lips and licks my blood off.

Yeah, he's definitely a psycho...

I roll my eyes in disgust, shaking my head, doing my best to not show my kidnapper that he is slowly winning.

"You taste just as sweet as I imagined. I can't wait to mark your beautiful backside even more." He stands a few paces back and practices small lashings in the air just mere inches away from my back. "Just to warn you now, I dipped the tip of this whip in hemlock and silver. Should make you hallucinate and burn your skin all at once. Are you ready to continue princess? Oh, do tell me when you've had enough, I wouldn't want you to black out again. Who knows what fun I might have to wake you up to." My kidnapper continues whipping my backside slowly before I even have a chance to respond.

Not that I can really find the words as each hit, each sting causes my vision to blur more and go red with pain and agony. Every hit just makes me dig my heels in harder as the hemlock and silver burn into my backside. He wants to crush me, he wants me to give in, to surrender. I just can't. I can't let him win; I won't submit.

I'll never let my spirit break, no matter what they do, I'll keep searching for strength within. No matter how beaten up I am, I'll find a way to push through. My life is not something they can take away from me. I will continue to fight and hold onto what is right with all my strength. Ultimately, it's that unwavering determination that will help me persevere.

With every slash on my back, the pain becomes more and more unbearable. My shackles dig into my skin as I squirm from the whipping; I've lost feeling in my arms and my back. With calculated precision, he pours a bucket of freezing water over me, shocking my body and mind into full alertness, amplifying the agony of the open wounds on my back.

Without a doubt, my kidnapper is finding pleasure in this situation. He uses burning herbs and tonics to torture me, resulting in hallucinations and a heightened libido. He constantly medicates me to prevent me from using magic and make me feel powerless. I don't know how long he continues on with this line of torture. Tears don't just blur my vision, they make it completely black from the pain. My body collapses, granting me a brief respite from his deranged actions.

***

In this abyss of torture and pain, time holds no significance.

The suffering continues endlessly, with each passing moment inflicting more and more excruciating pain. In this room, my screams resonate, composing a bone-chilling symphony of torment. As time goes by, I feel myself falling further into despair, my resolve weakening, like a candle on the verge of being snuffed out.

I'm overwhelmed with the belief that I will never escape this situation. The darkness has become a cherished friend, offering me solace from the cruelty.

Until I'm awakened by a rhythmic movement and a fire burning deep within my core, causing my sex to burn. My back feels like it is on fire as the fabrics dig and reopen my wounds. My limbs are so heavy from being chained, that it takes too much strength to lift them to realize that I am not chained to the wall. The rhythmic movements because hard and forceful, I feel like I'm being ripped from the inside out. His grip on my hips dig in harder, leaving more bruises on my body.

I take a risk and open my eyes, as best as I can, my kidnapper's brutality has bruised and battered my face.

"Ah, good morning there sleeping beauty!" My eyes do not deceive me in the slightest. He grips me hard and thrusts harder and deeper into my sex. My arms are chained to the headboard of the bed, I give a couple of light tugs, which proves futile.

The pain. Unbearable.

But something worse deep inside me ignites as I am pinned beneath this beast. I feel my body betray me as he rapes my body and soul, my orgasm almost within sight. My kidnapper feels this need from my body, he feels my body's fire roaring to life, and my sex gripping his cock as I climb closer to the climax.

I fight my body's urge. I dig my fingernails into my palms tightly, blood slowly trickling out from beneath my fingers. My kidnapper thrusts faster, deeper, and harder until he finishes, his seed emptying into my sex. The thought instantly sickens me and brings me back, my body reeling back from the edge of climax. He withdraws his cock from my sex, his seed spilling out of me and dripping between my legs on the bed.

My kidnapper stands up, cleans himself, and gets dressed quickly, all while my soul breaks from his invasion. No, his violation. His violation of my body breaks me in more ways than I imagine. I curl my legs up to my stomach, attempting to hide myself from him, from his eyes that are filled with hunger and torment. Tears fill my eyes once more, running down my cheeks, like my soul leaving my body the only way it can.

He turns towards me, leans over, and grabs the bottom of my chin, pinching my cheeks and planting a forceful kiss on my lips. "You taste as good as you felt wrapped around my cock princess. I'll be having you more later, don't you worry about that." He turns and leaves, the door slamming shut and locking me in the room. Leaving me alone in my own personal hell. The tears pour out of me like a waterfall.

I need to get out of here.
I need to find a way to escape.
I need my magic...

***

Time drags on, I can't recall how many blackouts I've experienced or how many days have passed; his torture continues without an end in sight. He alternates between chaining me up against the wall and chained down to the bed. His brutality is relentless and the marks he leaves on my body are a constant reminder of my torment, a painful reminder of the ordeal that I have to endure. Every minute that goes by seems like an endless cycle of suffering, as the hours merge together. I have lost track of how long I've been locked away in this room, how long it has been since I last saw Brody.

My mind is a battleground of constant anguish, fear, and pain. The only solace I find is when he goes away following the act of rape; his torment echoes within me like a broken record.

Whipping.

Bleeding

Groping.

Degradation.

Rape.

Darkness.

Repeat.

Amidst the encroaching darkness of this hell, my spirit is splintered, desperately holding on to one thought that shines through as a guiding light.

I will see Shadow again, somehow, I will see him again.

My kidnapper has left me for some time now, though he leaves me chained to this grungy excuse of a bed. My soul screams to find the strength to break free. Though my body is weak and broken, I beg the Goddess to help me summon the last remnants of my strength and resolve.

Pushing aside the agony, overwhelmed by desperation, I summon my last surge of bravery and determination springing into action. Overwhelmed by desperation, I summon an intense surge of determination, breaking free from the chains, my wrists painfully raw and bleeding.

I manage to push myself up in the bed; my limbs shaky, unsteady, and extremely heavy as I attempt to stand. Nausea and lightheadedness from pain and dehydration wreak havoc within me, causing me to stumble to the door. Testing the doorknob, I quickly realized that my kidnapper had failed to secure it.

Hope...

I gently pull the door open, being careful not to make any noise that might expose my one chance. As I stumble through dim corridors, the drugs in my veins numb my senses, each step feels like exploring unfamiliar territory. Walking on the debris-covered floor feels like stepping on freezing shards, the chilly wind a constant reminder of my exposed state.

The surroundings become hazy and indistinct, making it hard to distinguish between what is real and what is a hallucination. Despite obstacles, my unwavering goal to escape fuels my determination to push forward.

Every second that goes by and every step I take, I feel my strength fading and my body becoming more fatigued and in pain. My mind is filled with countless questions and fears as I navigate through the maze of these hallways.

Will I find a way out?

Will I ever see the light of day again?

Will I ever see his face again?

Right when everything appears hopeless, a distant glint of light catches my tired eyes in the hallway's distance. With newfound resolve, I limp towards it, staying hidden in the shadows, my steps uncertain but resolute. As I approach, the light morphs into a breathtaking view of the city skyline, visible through a broken window.

Looking out the window, my suspicions are confirmed; I am in the Warehouse district and this fortress is guarded by numerous vampires. This abundant force is overwhelming to see, each one patrolling the rooftops of several buildings surrounding this one.

No wonder I haven't been rescued, there is just no way that anyone would be able to get to me unnoticed.

Closing my eyes, searching deep within myself, and using the last of my strength, I call forth my magic. Within a few seconds, my call is answered, and a purple orb of energy appears before me, my hero is this whisp.

Oh, thank the Goddess!

"Miss Spellcaster, how may I be of service?" The orb questions me without hesitation.

"I need you to carry a message to my familiar, Shadow. I don't know where he is right now, and I have no way of paying for this message. I used the last of my reserves to summon you. I'm desperate, and it's urgent! I'm being held captive, being tortured. GO! You MUST find him!" I plead with the whisp.

Before I can say more, the whisp vanishes, my only hope is that it will deliver my message to Shadow. I feel like Princess Leia from Star Wars, begging for Obi-Wan Kenobi's help.

"Hey, YOU!" A figure at the end of the hallway yells out, pointing at me. My adrenaline surges as I recognize the figure as one of the Queen's vampires. I take off running, opposite of the vampire, trying to avoid any large debris and glass littering the floor. I hear thunderous footsteps gain on me within a matter of seconds. I don't know why I even bothered trying to outrun a vampire.

Hands and arms snaked around my stomach, lifting me up off my feet, and pulling me up against the firm figure. I kick and thrash all my limbs, throwing my weight to break free, even if it is futile.

"You might as well give up already, you're weak, I'm a vampire. You're no match for me, maybe if you had magic..." A deep masculine voice states in my ear before throwing me up over his shoulder.

I know he's right, but there is just something inside me begging me to not give up. I need to believe that the whisp is going to get to Shadow and that he will find a way to me. That is what keeps me going. I stop fighting him, not because I know he is right, but because I need to save my strength.

The Queen's vampire walks down the halls, familiar and not all at the same time. I can't make heads or tails of where we are going until he walks through those set of double doors leading to the center of the Nest. Back in front of the Queen. The vampire kneels before the Queen, head bowed out of loyalty and respect, sending me falling onto the cold floor naked. The fall reawakens the pain and damage inflicted on my body, my wounds rip open up again from the sudden movement.

"What do we have here Logan?" The Queen leans forward on her throne, preening at my injured state.

The vampire, Logan, looks up from his kneeled state, "She was attempting to escape my Queen."

"Ahh, well we can't have that now, can we?" Her voice expressing her joy over my disobedience. She turns her head and motions for Declan, who flies to her side. She whispers something to him and he leaves. I can only imagine that she has demanded for Brody to be brought before us once again.

The Queen continues to have a conversation with Logan, praising him for his loyalty to her, flirting with him about how he caught me and dutifully brought me to her; the vampire is enraptured with how much attention that the Queen is giving him that he doesn't see she could kill him without blinking twice. I'm completely ignored like I'm insignificant lying here on the floor barely alive. I curl myself up in a ball attempting to hide my naked form, I may be almost dead, but I still have my dignity.

Brody is brought in a few moments later, looking just as worse for wear as I am. He's dropped to the floor next to me, barely alive. I turn my face to make eye contact with him, he's barely able to open one eye. The other eye is swollen shut, his wounds are still fresh and bleeding beneath him, creating reflective puddles on the floor. He won't be able to last too much longer.

Oh, Brody. Hang in there.

We will find a way out of this.

Our bodies, physically abused by these monsters, show suffering - wounds, burns, including bruises. The Queen leans forward as the door behind us opens and my kidnapper walks in, still elusive as ever wearing his mask, the energy in the room instantly changes as he sees me lying on the floor.

"Well, thank you for finally joining us my love. I hope you can answer how your plaything managed to ALMOST escape?" The Queen's condescending tone escalates to almost a yell, vibrating off the walls of the room.

My kidnapper walks to the steps of the Dias, kneels, and bows his head, completely walking by me without making any eye contact. "My apologies my Queen. It seems that she has been burning through the drug quicker than I anticipated, I didn't wish for her to die of an overdose."

The Queen considers his response for a few moments, before descending down off her throne, practically gliding with elegance to stand before my kidnapper. She bends down and grabs him by his throat, lifting him up from his knees to his toes barely skimming the floor. His hands instinctively reach up to grab at the Queen's grip, struggling to regain his breath control.

"Do you need to be reminded of all that is at stake?" Her anger towards him unrelenting.

"N-no." He manages to slip out while trying to gasp for air. The Queen releases him, letting him drop to the floor. He quickly regains his composure, straightening his outfit out and walking towards us.

"Take care of this mess, my love. Their presence is bothersome." She waves her hands at us like we are garbage to be taken out.

"For play or for disposal my Queen?" He asks her just as he stands before us, looking down at us as if we are nothing more than husks of empty shells.

All I hear for her response is one that makes my kidnapper chuckle as he grabs me by the ankle, dragging me across the stone-cold floor. I attempt to grab at the floor, trying to delay the inevitable as much as I can. He drags me all of two feet before—

BOOM!

A thunderous boom shakes the walls of the building, causing debris to fall from the ceiling, everyone pausing in their tracks. The Queen orders several of her vampires to go assess the damage to the building and to find out what the hell is going on. Declan immediately approaches the Queen, forcing her behind him, for he knows that without her they will be lost. Several other vampires swarm at the bottom steps of the Dias, forming a vampire-made wall.

Screams of pain and agony are heard on the other side of the double doors. Sounds of fighting, yelling, and gunshots going off can be heard in the distance. My kidnapper drags me back to Brody's lifeless body and takes ranks to the many vampires that have come to protect their Queen, along with several other masked assailants, pushing us behind them.

After a few moments, the double doors open, and an injured vampire walks forward. I can barely make out, through the vampires in front of me, that Galen, Shadow, and several other werewolves have entered after slowly. They move cautiously, knowing that each step they take is a risk to their lives.

Just when they are about 20 feet away from the ring of vampires, Galen rushes forward and stabs his hand through the back of the injured vampire. The garbled sound that the vampire makes right before Galen rips his hand back out with the vampire's heart, is unsettling. Galen purposefully drops the heart in full view of the Queen, only adding fuel to her already raging self. The heart falling to the floor, and the squish as it lands echoes throughout the room, escalating the tension almost instantly.

"HOW DARE YOU COME INTO MY NEST WOLF!" The Queen's shouting reverberates through the room, sending chills down my spine. Galen not impressed by her demeanor, continues to stand there meeting her glare with daggers of his own.

"You took something of mine. I want it back!" He shouts, taking a single step forward, Shadow right on his heels snarling towards them all.

The Queen steps out from behind Declan and slowly starts to descend down the stairs. I know this is a trap and I'm just too weak to warn them all about it. The silence is deafening and unsettling. I can feel my heartbeat and it sounds like it's going to pop out of my chest. The pain from my wounds only adds to the throbbing heartbeat like pain ripping through my body.

The Queen leans down and grabs me by the back of my neck, lifting me up off the floor with ease. Lifting me up off the ground, exposing my naked body to not only Galen, but everyone in the room to see the torture that has been inflicted on me.

And my view of him.

In my weakened state, I can make out that not only did Shadow and Galen come to my rescue, but so did Dizzy and my Dad, who happens to be in wolf form. I would recognize my Dad in wolf form any day. He has more red than gray striping on his coat and his form is just as large as Galen is.

Shadow snarls as his view of me becomes clearer. *"Callie..."*

I hear his mind-link, but I'm just too weak to answer. I start crying, not just from hearing him, but from the Queen's painful grip.

"I-I'm sorry Shadow..." My cry intensifies and tears explode down my face like a dam giving away. The Queen squeezes the back of my neck harder, causing me to flinch more.

"STOP!" Galen's voice is loud and thunderous, his fists clenched so tight that they turn white with rage.

The Queen looks Galen dead in the eyes, "You want her? Come and get her!" She throws me off to the side, forcing me to land painfully on my back, causing more of my wounds to re-open and drain fresh blood. The metallic smell starts to create a frenzy among the vampires.

I gasp from the pain and in that moment several things happen at once. My Dad leaps towards the nearest vampire and rips his head clean off. Bones crunching and liquid splattering break the silence. Galen attempts to rush forward but is blocked when my kidnapper unleashes his magic, hitting Galen with a blast so powerful that it knocks him back to the ground. The rest of the pack werewolves unleash their primal fury, tearing through the ranks of the vampires and masked assailants with ferocious strength and agility.

I start to slowly make my way towards Brody; each movement as painful as the next as I try to slide towards him unnoticed.

In the midst of chaos, Shadow, Galen, Dizzy, and my Dad fight relentlessly, strategizing every move to reach us and ensure our freedom. Every step they take presents them with formidable opponents, forcing them to test their skill and bravery against impossible odds.

But even through the fighting I can see that both sides are losing members of both nest or pack, bodies start to litter the floor, blood pooling all around us. Lives are lost in the heat of battle, brave souls falling in defense of their friends and allies. Yet, through it all, they press on, driven by a singular purpose: to rescue me and Brody at any cost.

The Queen's forces seem to be matched equally to that of the werewolves. The atmosphere is filled with intense anticipation as fists clash and claws tear through flesh in a chaotic and violent battle of blood and steel. Every move becomes a deadly dance of death as they battle against overwhelming odds.

As time goes on, the conflict escalates, lives are at stake, and the pack's future hangs in the balance. The battle echoes through the chamber, blending with the cries of the injured and the unleashed magic's roar.

Refusing to surrender, the werewolves and vampires persist against each other at all odds. They continue with unwavering determination, pushing deeper into the heart of darkness. They realize that their bravery is not determined by their ability to avoid conflict, but by their determination to confront it directly, all for the sake of their loved ones.

Warm hands cup the sides of my face, I look up to see Dizzy's bright green eyes staring deep into me. "Callie, we need to go. You have to get up." She encourages me as she helps me get up off the cold ground, hanging on to me around the waist, throwing my arm up around her shoulders. She is definitely stronger than she looks for her size.

"We can't leave Brody..." I plea with her, reaching out toward him. She knows that I would never leave him behind. He's here because of me, they just don't know it.

Dizzy locks eyes with one of the pack werewolves and motions for them to collect Brody's body. The wolf comes over, grabs Brody's arm, and slowly drags him towards the door as Dizzy starts to help me walk. The fighting is out of control, blood everywhere screams echoing, and bodies pile up as more werewolves fall. It's clear that if something is not done quickly the wolves are going to lose and we will never escape. I scan the fighting and lay eyes that Declan and Galen are in a heated match, both have blood dripping from several threatening wounds.

Shadow, sensing the same conclusion, confronts the masked assailant, my kidnapper, with blood dripping from his mouth, throwing a vampire's head to the floor. With his golden eyes ablaze with determination, his ragged breaths from battle, and his sleek black fur bristling with tension, he faces his opponent with every muscle primed for the upcoming challenge.

Surrounded by the chaos of the battle, Shadow and my kidnapper exchange a silent look that conveys their determination and resistance. They share an intense understanding, recognizing the roles they must assume in this deadly game.

Shadow springs forward, growling menacingly, his sharp claws gleaming like daggers in the chamber's dim light. There is a head-on collision between my kidnapper and Shadow, causing shockwaves to ripple through the air.

Time appears to freeze as they exchange powerful blows with an almost insane intensity. Desperation and determination fuel each strike as they fiercely battle for an advantage. Despite Shadow's ability to hold his ground against my kidnapper, we both understand that he cannot escape this fight without being harmed. Shadow pauses for just a moment, finds me amongst the fighting, and locks eyes with me.

"I love you..."

His mind-link barely a whisper, as Shadow summons all of his remaining strength, and charges straight on at my kidnapper. Shadow's enormous figure engulfs the masked assailant as he crumples to the ground from the blow's impact. In this moment, our familiar bond snaps, breaking like a mirror being shattered into a million pieces. I panic as I don't see Shadow move. Instead, my kidnapper pushes the massive unmoving form to the side, standing up and holding a dagger. A dagger dripping in blood.

The realization hits and the pain of the familiar bond dissipating becomes unbearable, yet understandable. Seeing his life slip away causes me to fall to my knees and my soul fills with every emotion.

No...

As if reawakening from a dream, I close my eyes and pull deep within myself all that I can summon. Pain, anger, despair, and rage are all fueling my body, pushing adrenaline through me, my magic just a flicker before is now a time bomb ticking.

My whole body is radiating a bright red aura as my magic burns through me. So many bodies; vampires and werewolves litter the ground. So much death, and for what?

For me?

"Callie, don't do it. Control yourself." His voice breaks through all the emotions I'm feeling, attempting to distract me and bring me back to reality. Galen, covered in blood and severe injuries that are draining him of his energy, is standing right in front of me, trying to push through my wall of magic.

"Galen...He killed Shadow...Shadow's g-gone...Sh-Shadow...it hurts. It all hurts. I can't stop it and I don't want it to stop." My voice shakes and my sobs are overthrown by my rage and despair, the red aura growing and firing out bits of electricity.

Understanding my pain and unwillingness to let it go, Galen quickly moves, grabbing Dizzy, Brody, and a few of the last remaining werewolves and ducking behind the double doors. Timed perfectly, I let go of it all.

All the hate.

All the rage.

All the pain.

All the torture.

I release my magic and it truly is a beautiful sight to behold. A brilliant wave of red energy burns everything, just like a bomb, leaving me whole in the center.

I don't know who I have killed in this moment or who escaped.

I don't care.

The one thing that mattered to me the most is gone.

My last thought before my world goes black.

I just hope I used enough magic and energy to join him in the Afterlife...

Sixteen

I AWAKE TO BIRDS chirping, bright sunlight everywhere, the soft grass beneath me tickling my legs, and the firm tree at my backside supporting me. I recognize the forest surrounding me that of pack territory; looking around, everything seems so surreal.

How did I get here?

"You're awake, about time." A feminine voice states behind me, causing me to jump out of my skin.

I get up from the grass, dusting the grass and leaves from me, peeking around the tree to see Maybelle standing there with her walking staff. Her aura looks bright and radiant as ever, a golden hue encasing her as if she never lost her magic.

"Maybelle?"

"Who else dear?" She replies simply with a smile. I rush over to her and hug her tight. The physical contact with her causes tears to pool down my face, I never thought I would see her again. Her warmth fills me up and reminds me that this must be a dream. I remember the events that happened before waking up here, being kidnapped, tortured, raped, Galen attempting to rescue us...

"Maybelle, am I dead? Is-is this the afterlife?" I stumble to get the words out, mostly out of fear of her answer and anger at myself for causing this all the happen.

As if reading my face, Maybelle grabs my hands in hers, looking up at me with her brilliant green eyes. "You're not dead, not exactly. Let's go take a walk, we have much to discuss." She holds her hand out to me, instinctively I clasp her hand knowing that wherever we are, I know I'm safe.

Walking with Maybelle through the forest is too surreal, it's as if time has gone backward. Maybelle is wearing her typical maxi dress in an ombré earth tone variety of colors and I stare down at myself to see that I'm wearing my usual dark blue jeggings, black tank top, and boots. It feels just like old times, except not.

"Maybelle, where are we? What's going on?" I'm eager to know what is going on. I need to know what happened.

"Before I answer that, I just have one question for you. What do you remember?"

I ponder her question.

I remember the pain.

Rage.

And...

Despair...

I remember casting a spell, with all my remaining magic and physical strength that I had left within me. As if realizing that I remember everything, Maybelle stops walking beside me, still holding my hand causing me to stop.

"We are in the Bridge. It's a parallel plane between the living world and the Afterlife. Some call it the Shadow plane." She explains. She tugs my hand forward as she starts to walk down the beaten path, urging me to continue walking with her.

We continue walking, her explaining all that is happening right now, and I listen, trying to process everything that she is saying. Galen rushed back in after I exploded my magic, rushing my unconscious body to the hospital, along with Brody. The Vampire Queen and Declan escaped. My kidnapper escaped,

Galen says that he must be a powerful witch or something because Galen saw him surrounded by a huge shield.

Meaning my spell was cast for nothing.

Continuing her explanation, Maybelle reveals that the doctors felt it was necessary to place me, and Brody, in medically induced comas at the hospital for healing purposes. I am currently in the ICU in critical condition, as a result of the injuries from the spell and the trauma inflicted by my kidnapper. Despite his vampire attributes, Brody's fast healing required sedation for mental recovery and stability.

I understand the importance of medically induced comas as a nurse since they provide our bodies with the needed time to heal and minimize further risks. It is a common approach when working with assault and trauma victims. Memories of my torture keep resurfacing, wondering if there's something I overlooked. I contemplate different actions I could have taken.

"There is nothing you could have done. You have no reason to blame yourself." Maybelle chimes in, interrupting my guilt trip.

Before I'm able to argue with her about my guilt, I'm interrupted by a deep masculine voice, "You cannot blame yourself, Callie."

I look ahead on the path ahead and see what I thought I never would again.

Shadow, in all of his massive glory.

I turn to Maybelle, smiling and letting go of her hand as I rush off to wrap my arms around Shadow. He feels just as he always has, warm, furry, and nothing but muscle. The minute I'm in his arms, I let go of all of the pain and rage.

Shadow whispers in my ear, telling me that my courage and my strength are all I need in this world. He encourages me that he has never been so proud of me, of being my familiar and guide, and of being my friend. I know this is our last goodbye, I don't want it to be, but it's already done. He's already gone, my kidnapper saw to that. The image of the dagger coated in his blood is still seared into my mind.

Tears blur my vision and start to roll down my cheeks, unwilling to say goodbye one last time to my best friend. As he keeps whispering in my ear, all I can do is nod and silently cry, knowing that there is nothing I can do anyway makes me feel helpless. Guilt floods through me, if I had never sent that whisp he never would have known where I was and there is a good chance that he would still be alive.

"It's time for us to go Shadow," Maybelle says quietly. I had almost forgotten that she was even there.

No...

This isn't fair.

This isn't how it is supposed to be.

I glance up, from holding onto my dear friend, to see Maybelle standing there in the middle of the forest path waiting for Shadow.

"Wait, what's going on?" I'm so confused. *Us?* I glance back to Shadow looking for an explanation of any kind.

Shadow looks at Maybelle, nodding in agreement. He looks back at me, "Maybelle and I are going to the Afterlife together."

His words his hard. I knew that he was dead, but Maybelle? When did that happen? Why didn't she tell me? My breathing and heart rate increase as panic starts to flow throughout my body.

Does this mean I'm going to the Afterlife?

"Callie, it's ok. Look at me. It's going to be ok." Shadow's voice soothes my panic almost instantly.

"How is it going to be ok? You're dead, I'll be alone and it's all my fault!" Panic bubbles over and I just melt right to the ground, falling to my knees. Shadow and Maybelle walk over to me and gather me up from the ground, both holding me.

Maybelle brings her hand to cup my face, "Child, you know that this is not the end. Remember your lessons from when you were my pupil. This is not the end. We will see each other again." She uses her thumb to wipe away a stray tear falling down my cheek.

Shadow dips his head low and scoops up my hand to rest on the top of his head. "I'll never truly leave you. Always."

We stand there for a moment, savoring the moment of our last moments together. I close my eyes and just breathe. Allowing their warmth and strength to fill me where I had felt cold and empty during my time with my kidnapper.

Slowly the warmth fades as I open my eyes to see them gone. I'm just standing there alone, in the middle of the forest.

Now what?

I start walking through the forest, making my way towards where I think the lake would be. I'm not really sure what to do now or how to even get out of here. This place is an exact replica of what the real world is, was, I'm not really sure what pretense to use because I have no idea if I'm going to return to it, be stuck here, or move on to the Afterlife. The lake comes into view and is exactly where it is supposed to be, but oddly the coloring of the lake is deeper. It's more clear and brighter than before.

"Oh, good. You found us." A masculine voice says from behind me, startling me. I quickly jump and turn around to see a man and woman standing there like a vision. Both of them look daunting; blonde hair, striking blue eyes, and toned body forms that suggest that they can handle themselves in a fight. The man wearing long flowing white pants and an open-chest dark tunic; while the woman is wearing a sparkling white floor-length slim dress. They both radiate such immense auras; I can only imagine that they have great powers.

"I-I...I'm sorry. Forgive me, but who are you?" I stammer to get my question out, almost afraid to know the answer.

The woman brings her fingers up to her mouth, chuckling and blushing, almost trying to hold back her amusement of my question. Anger flickers for a second, as I don't appreciate being treated like an idiot.

"Excuse us, we should have introduced ourselves." The man steps forward and brings his hand to his chest. "My name is Helios, and this is my sister Selene." He waves over towards the woman.

Those names.

I remember those names from my lessons.

Holy Gods and Goddesses!

I must look like an idiot as I work through my thoughts to realize that I'm actually standing in front of a real God and Goddess. I start to bow before them.

"Please, don't do that. It's not necessary." The Goddess rushes forward, with speed faster than a vampire, quickly grabbing my hands and stopping me from finishing my bow and paying respect.

Selene, standing in front of me, her voice is soft and gentle. "As you know, you are in a coma. My brother and I heard your call during that last spell you cast. Honestly, that spell was very impressive. So impressive that my brother and I would like to help you."

"Help me? Why? How? I'm so confused." I take my hands out of her grip carefully so as to not offend their courtesy. I take a step back cautiously; this is just so much to process.

"Slowly Selene, let's not overwhelm the poor girl. We need to gain her trust and give her answers before we do anything else." Helios reminds his sister.

The resemblance between the two is uncanny. It's almost as if they are twins. From what I remember from my lessons, Selene is the moon Goddess and Helios is the sun God. Both are extremely powerful and revered by all supernaturals. Selene nods to her brother and walks towards the bank of the lake, taking a seat in the soft grass.

"Callie, come sit with me. This is going to take a while." She pats the grass next to her, insisting I follow her lead. I look back at Helios; he extends his hand out toward the direction of his sister, following her lead to take a seat as well.

"Do you remember what happened to you?" Helios asks as he takes a seat next to me, sandwiching me between the two of them.

I remember everything.

Anger flares inside me as all the memories flash through my mind. I pull my knees up to my chest, holding on to my arms in a death grip, my knuckles turning white.

Selene lays a sympathetic hand on my shoulder, her warmth gravitating to me, attempting to settle my nerves. "We never meant for any of that to happen to you. It's not what my brother and I had planned for you. We...apologize for all the pain that you endured. And I apologize for not being able to answer your cries for help." Her words astonish me, I'd never thought I would ever see the day when a Goddess would apologize for anything. I had always thought that my lessons with Maybelle about the Gods and Goddess were pointless; I never realized that they still existed.

"You've endured so much Callie. My sister and I would like to offer you a chance to decide what happens next. Keep in mind, that whatever decision you make is of your own accord and cannot changed. Your decision will also determine how you live your new life." Helios's statement is overwhelming as I sit there, trying to process what he is saying.

I get to decide my own fate.

I get the chance to change my fate.

Selene and Helios offer me various choices that could impact my life. Their words compel me to reflect on the implications of my decisions and the course I wish to follow.

I am conflicted by the options before me, each leading to a distinct life journey. I feel like my mind is going to burst from the information that's been presented. While discussing various options, they almost disregard my presence. I find myself throwing my hands up in frustration due to the sheer magnitude of this life-altering decision.

"I-I need a moment. I need to think about all this." I get up from the grass and start to walk off into the woods. My mind racing with all the options and possibilities. I keep walking, pushing myself deeper into the forest until I'm panting and sweating.

I fall to my knees, out of breath, feeling completely out of my mind. How do I make a decision like this?

Everything will be ok...

Shadow's voice fills my head, silencing all the problems bouncing around in my head. Closing my eyes, I focus on my breathing. Once my breathing settles, my heart rate slows, and my mind is finally able to start processing all that Selene and Helios are offering me.

If I knew the outcome, making choices would be much easier; I guess that's why they say hindsight is 20/20. Reflecting on their words, my mind is unraveling with possibilities. The choices I make will have an impact on those in my vicinity.

My first choice allows me to return to my normal life. Being a nurse at Capital City Hospital and living in the same house would seem like the simplest choice to make. However, the caveat would be that my memory would be completely erased of all things supernatural in relation to myself. I will be human, no longer a witch, or be able to practice magic. I'll still retain all knowledge of Brody and Galen as colleagues only and nothing more. Along with not having access to magic, I will lose my werewolf traits and live a normal life, as well as aging a human as well.

The second choice has me returning to my original state, which is currently lying in a coma at the hospital where I work at. I get to retain my status as a witch and have access to magic. Along with being a witch, I'll become the first-ever witch-were-wolf hybrid. Helios and Selene let it slip that I should have become one already, however when they sent Shadow to me to become my familiar it suppressed my hybrid instincts. Helios says that if I choose to become a hybrid, there will be much more for me to discover about my past. The life I had been living has been a half lie and it will be up to me to discover the truth.

The last choice is even simpler; I would get to go on to the Afterlife. What was it that Spike said to Buffy in that Vampire Slayer show, "Death is easy, it's living that is hell?" The Afterlife does seem like an easy choice, almost too easy though. I have never been one to take the easy way out on anything.

How does one choose their own destiny without really know-ing the outcome? I know that each decision has its own con-sequence and will shape my life and those around me. Could I really embrace a human life? Would being human really offer me a simpler life? Would I be happy with a simpler life? A life just fo-cused on being a nurse and having normal human relationships? Living a life blended into human society and without the chal-lenges or dangers of that the supernatural seems almost...boring.

Can I really turn my back on all that I have ever known and done? What about my life has been a half-lie? Can I truly be happy returning to my life at this present moment? Memories of being kidnapped, tortured, and raped repeat like a broken record in my mind. Can I truly heal from all this trauma? Es-pecially since I will be returning to a world without Shadow and Maybelle? Can I truly go back to my relationships with Brody and Galen without them treating me like a victim? Like

I'm damaged goods? The bonds and memories that I've created with both men go just as deep as the bond and trauma inflicted by my kidnapper. Would it just be easier to wipe it all away and start over with a clean slate?

My identity has always revolved around embracing my magical and werewolf heritage. Is it possible that this is the half-lie mentioned by Helios? Can I truly resume my normal life, despite the realization that I've been living a lie? Being a witch has always given me purpose, and having werewolf traits only intensified it. However, becoming a hybrid would be a major adjustment. What would it even mean to be a hybrid? All I know is that it will be tough to navigate this path on my own.

But will I truly be alone?

"No, you won't." Selena's voice behind me breaks my internal monologue, causing me to look over my shoulder. She's standing there a few feet away and answered my question. "I'm sorry, I don't mean to rush you, but we are running out of time. You can't stay here for long. We need to know what your decision is."

"You said I won't be alone. How do you know this? I haven't made a decision yet."

"We never have any intention of sending you back alone. Not completely anyway. We have ways of sending you back with something, no matter which choice you make." Selene turns to the side and standing behind her is the most beautiful, white wolf I've ever seen.

The fur glistening like diamonds in the sun, or new fallen snow. I rise from the ground and turn to greet this majestic creature. The wolf walks towards me, as it draws closer, I see that its size is about the same as Galen when he is in his wolf form. Her movements are soft, not tampering with the ground beneath her paws.

'My name is Eve, I'm your wolf...'

Her voice is soft and feels like a whisper in my head. In this moment, time stops as I raise my hand to feel her fur. The moment my hand touches her fur, a warm tingling sensation radiates from my hand up my arm.

She is my wolf.

She is me.

Looking into her golden eyes is like looking into a mirror. Her spirit is calm and wild. Her presence instantly calms me as Shadow once did. In this moment, meeting her solidifies my decision; this is going to be a life-changing experience, one that I hope that I can adapt to. Looking at my wolf, makes me feel like I can conquer the world.

I look up at Selene, and she nods her head towards me, understanding my decision.

Seventeen

P AIN...

So much pain.

I am in a state of agony that encompasses both emotional and physical pain. The simple act of moving my fingers is enough to make my body scream and burn with fire. I'm too afraid to open my eyes right now.

I'm fearful of discovering what happened while I was in a state of unconsciousness. Afraid to know the physical state of my body. Afraid of the looks that will be given to me after knowing what happened to me.

And the stench is unbearable. Do all hospitals smell like this? Or is this just a side effect of becoming a hybrid? I don't know if I'm ever going to be able to work in this hospital again. The smell of decay and death permeates through my sinuses, causing a wave of nausea to hit, making my stomach curl.

'You can't hide forever Callie. You need to wake up and accept your new fate...' Eve's voice echoes inside me; I reach inside me and feel her presence. I have made a choice; I need to accept it and carry on, I just can't help but want to hide just a little bit longer.

'Ok, fine. But I need your strength, everything hurts. Just moving my fingers feels like fire.' I reach out to her in my center, finding her there sitting proudly, waiting for me to reach out and accept her strength as my own.

I curl my left hand into a fist and stretch my fingers back out. I can hear hushed voices as if people are trying to whisper, but little do they know, I can hear everything.

"Did the doctor say when she was going to wake up?"

"Did you see all the scars on her back?"

"They said that she almost died..."

Chuckling to myself, I'm unsure if the whispers are from inside the room or outside in the hallway. If I had to guess, I'd say the nurses are gossiping in the hallway, eager to enter this room. Brace yourselves for a terrifying awakening people, this witch isn't done with this world just yet...Or should I say this hybrid isn't done with this world just yet?

Thanks to my heightened senses, I can also perceive the heartbeats of three people who are gathered near me. Through my magical abilities, I can visualize everything in my head, even if it's just a tiny bit. Beside me, Brody is peacefully sleeping in a chair, while my parents are huddled together on the other side of the room. Their leaning toward each other brings about a sense of worry that leaves a terrible taste in my mouth, yet simultaneously provides a reassuring anchor for the chaotic moments ahead.

I curl and stretch my fingers on my other hand when I notice something very soft in the bed with me. As I go to wiggle my toes, I feel a heavy weight lying across my legs. I move my fingers over the softness of my bed.

Fur?

Who the hell is in the bed with me?

Why am I weighted down?

Reaching out with my magic once more, I can feel the powerful aura, an Alpha aura. I can see the outline of his aura revealing a massive wolf in my bed with me, lying across my legs and feet. He keeps constant watch over me, which I find oddly endearing and alarming at the same time. It's as if he's afraid that I won't make it through this. His action reminds me of something that Shadow would be doing, being my silent protector.

Galen.

But why is he in wolf form?

Pulling my magic back to me, curling my fingers once more, and feeling less pain than just a moment ago. It's time, I know it is, I can be like this forever. Time to rip off the bandaid.

My eyelids flutter open, and I squint so tightly as the bright brilliant light blinds me and causes an unimaginable head pain. Instinctively I bring my hands up to my head and eyes as I adjust to the harsh reality of light. My arms and hands feel like heavy weights as I use them instinctively to shield my eyes.

"Can someone turn off the lights? And close the blinds?" My question comes out as a whisper and hoarse from my mouth and my throat being dry.

Several things happen at once; everyone starts shouting all at once, my parents rush to my bedside, Brody uses his vampire speed to turn off the lights, and the giant wolf in my bed nearly crushes me as he attempts to lick all over my face. Mom and Dad fuss at Galen to back off so that they can see me, touch me, and hold me.

"Oh, Callie! Honey!"

"Galen, get off her already!"

"Brody, get the doctor!" My Dad shouts with as much excitement as I've ever seen a grown man have. Brody, not even hesitating, rushes out the door to find the doctor. I didn't even get a chance to say hello to him.

"Galen, I'm fine. Please stop, you're heavy. Get down!" I wave my hands at him, shouting to get him to cease, and he instinctively sits on his hindquarters, in between my feet, at the end of the bed. Wagging his tail, with his tongue hanging out of his mouth, he's by far the biggest lap dog ever.

With Galen finally off of me, I can finally breathe.

I gaze up at my parents. Mom's tears fall like a leaking faucet as she clings to my hands with a tight grip. Whether it's to remind her or myself, the pain of her grip assures me of my presence in reality, outside of dreams or the Shadow plane. Behind Mom stands Dad, clutching her shoulders. I have a feeling that if he releases her, she'll completely break down. He has always been her anchor.

Like Shadow was for me.

Shadow.

My face instantly sours at the thought that I know he's gone. I can't help but feel an immense wave of grief fill me. I push away some of the grief, I don't have the capacity to start to deal with my grief just yet.

I wonder if they know that Maybelle has also passed on.

"Water?" I croak out my plea to help get rid of this desert in my mouth and throat. My Dad pours me a small amount of water into a cup, places the straw to my lips, holding the cup for me. The water is so cold and feels like razor blades going down my esophagus that I start choking. Dad immediately takes the cup and straw away.

"Sorry baby, let's wait to see what the doctor says." My Mom squeezes my hand again. I give her a weak smile and start to assess myself and my injuries.

My right arm is supported by a pillow and encased in a cast, immobilized for safety, just like my left lower leg. My back feels like it's burning, likely scarred from the torture of being whipped and cut with a poisoned silver knife. My other arm is marked with bruises and cuts in different stages. My face feels battered from a wrestling match and the drug-induced brain fog is making it difficult to understand anything.

I attempt to shift in bed, grimacing at the sharp pain throbbing throughout my whole body, causing me to be nauseous from the pain.

GRRRR!

Galen growls at me and I just glare right back. I stop moving because in all reality there is just no point in moving. Between the pain, two separate cast limbs, and the big wolf in my bed, there just isn't any room left in the bed.

"How long have I been here?" Such a simple question, but something tells me that I'm going to be rather shocked by the answer.

"Four weeks precisely." A voice answers from the doorway.

I look over to see Brody has returned and brought the doctor with him. Dr. Samantha Perkins, short and stout, and full of piss and vinegar. I've had the pleasure of working with her many times, and each time was never a fun experience. But she happens to be one of the best female trauma doctors that this hospital has, older than most doctors here but is full of too much knowledge to retire just yet, so I know that I should be thankful to have her on my team.

"I'm going to overlook the fact that animals are not allowed in this facility based on the fact that I know who it is." Dr. Perkins just glares at Galen, approaching the bed cautiously. Dr. Perkins being human, doesn't miss a beat. She has been taking care of supernaturals long before they were ever announced to society, which makes her one of the few to trust in this hospital. She looks back at me with a sympathetic smile, "You're quite lucky. Your injuries were quite extensive; most we were able to correct quickly. I'm sorry that we had to put you..."

"In a coma," I whisper. "I know."

Dr. Perkins cocks her head slightly to the side, confused with how I would know such a thing before anyone has had a chance to tell me.

I explain to them all about how I was in the Bridge, with Shadow and Maybelle. Galen whines over this, which makes me think that he already knew that Maybelle had passed but didn't want to say anything. I go in depth over the details of what happened there and the choices that Helios and Selene offered to me.

I don't reveal to any of them that I'm a hybrid now, even though Eve insists that I tell them. I silence her by letting her know that now is not the time. I don't know when I will tell them, but I think it's not relevant at the moment and not pertinent to my recovery.

Dr. Perkins listens to everything I say, taking notes frivolously on her clipboard, and asking questions when appropriate; I think she can tell that I'm withholding back some crucial information. Then after a few moments of silence, she suggests starting with ice chips until I can swallow without choking. She states that she is limiting my allotment of visitors to two now that I'm fully awake.

Brody managed to slink out and back into the room with a cup of ice chips and a spoon. Handing the cup to me, my right hand instinctively grasps the cup but drops it, spilling ice chips all over the bed. Weakness and throbbing pain radiate up my whole right arm; instinctively I reach over my body to grab the fallen cup and ice chips and pain explodes throughout my back twisting. I grimace trying to hide the pain.

"Callie, I'm so sorry!" Brody rushes forward and starts picking up the ice chips. Mom and Dad rush forward to help pick up ice chips and get me back into a comfortable position. Galen growls in Brody's direction, Brody puts his hands up in surrender.

These two are going to be the death of me.

"It's ok Brody. It's not your fault." His apology is totally unnecessary, I should have known better than to grab it with my right hand and then try to correct myself with my left. I'm just a hot mess from all this.

Dr. Perkins clears her throat, all of us stop what we are doing and look over to her. "Sorry to interrupt, I just have a few more things that I need to review with Callie...Alone" She pauses before saying alone, eyeing everyone in the room including Galen.

Galen taking the hint, leans forward and licks my cheek, then huffs and shakes himself causing fur to fly everywhere before jumping off the bed. Dad tugs Mom by the elbow, she squeezes my hand one more time and gives me a small smile before allowing Dad to lead her out of my room. Brody leans forward gently and kisses my forehead, Galen growls. All I can do is roll my eyes at their level of testosterone.

Once everyone is gone, Dr. Perkins sits gently on my bed. I've never seen this side of her before. Her face shows sadness and worry, while the energy she is giving off is fear.

'Fear of what? Of me, why?

"Dr. Perkins, you're starting to scare me a little bit. Just spit it out already. I can handle it." Well, I least I think I can anyway. Isn't that what the little blue engine says?

Dr. Perkins clears her throat again. "Sorry, so ummm I need to collect a detailed recollection from you about what happened. From what Shadow and Brody told us, you were held captive for about a week. The state that you were brought in here was completely astonishing. I'm honestly, and thankfully, surprised that you are alive.

"The police are also going to want to talk with you, however, I was able to pull some strings and if you're willing to let me video record our conversation with a true stone, then they will take that as your statement and only come talk to you if they have more questions. I told them that the fewer people around during your immediate recovery, the better."

Dr. Perkins' level of empathy exceeds all standards. It doesn't matter why, but she's treating me with more kindness than any other victim, and I'm okay with that. I prefer to wait until I fully comprehend the scope of my newfound hybrid abilities.

I nod in agreement with her and we schedule a session to talk with a S.A. therapist for later on this morning. She says that she wants to do this while the memories are still fresh in my mind like I could never ever forget what has happened to me. She scribbles a few things down on her clipboard before getting up and leaving the room. Leaving me to my own thoughts.

It's the first time I can breathe freely since I woke up. Despite the pain, I am able to breathe. One of the nurses comes in to check on me and my IVs; I don't know who she is, but from how she doesn't come too close and her rapid heartbeat, she reeks of fear. Must be human and a new nurse at that. She engages in courteous conversation while present, but promptly excuses herself. My gaze follows her out the doorway, I see my parents talking with Dr. Perkins in hushed tones. Their expressions are a mix of worry and relief. When they notice me, their faces light up with a blend of joy and concern, as if I can't feel what they are.

'You know, if you want to hear what they are saying, all you have to do is concentrate...' Eve's voice whispers the ingenious idea into my head.

You know, she has a point. Taking advantage of being alone, I close my eyes and focus my concentration on what I can hear.

"Will she be ok?" Mom's voice shakes.

"As I've told you both before until I know the extent of what she went through, I can't honestly say. She is awake, it's a step in the right direction. Let's just take it one step at a time. She needs to rest. To heal." Dr. Perkins keeps her cool, which I can't imagine my parents are making it easy for her.

I open my eyes and let their voices fade; I don't need to hear any more right now. My parents are experiencing what I've seen other families of SA victims experience, grief and fear. Fear that I won't be the same as I was before, and they are right, I won't be.

I'm a hybrid now, and there is no going back.

Eve sends me a burst of warm energy. *'Thank you, Callie. I'm glad that you chose to accept me as your wolf.'*

A smile spreads across my face as I mentally accept her words, leaning my head against the soft pillows. I briefly shut my eyes, then feel someone else's presence at the doorway. As soon as I thought I could finally have some peaceful moments, the gentle scent of coffee and sandalwood fills the air.

"Hello, Forest," I say aloud, without opening my eyes.

"How did you know it was me?" His voice deep and smooth, used to melt my insides, but since my trauma, causes me to stand alert.

I smile and open my eyes to see him standing in the doorway, uniform in all, holding onto a bouquet of wildflowers. Looks like he picked them out himself, no plastic holding them together, just some twine. "I could smell you."

Blushing a little, Forest steps into the room and sets the flowers on the bedside table by the window. At which I notice that the table is covered with other bouquets and various cards. I don't know why I didn't notice before.

'Probably because you haven't had a moment of peace since you've woken up silly...' Eve butts in. And she's right, she's definitely my wolf for sure. Cheeky and spunky, just like me.

"I just wanted to check in on you. I heard that you woke up and rushed right over. My Captain won't let me work on your case; said I'm too personally involved..." Forest looks down at the floor, stuffing his hands in his pockets.

"Thank you, I'm doing ok. Well as ok as anyone in my situation I guess. I umm...just have to take one thing at a time, you know. Baby steps." I explain. I don't want to go into too much detail with him, he's a friend. I'm just not ready to talk it over with him or Galen; not yet anyway. I can feel myself filling with emotions, too many all at once. Anger, fear, grief, pain...

'Easy Callie, just breathe...' Eve attempts to calm me down. *'He needs to leave, something is wrong...'*

Sensing my discomfort and a sudden rush of emotions, my eyes well up in frustration; Forest apologizes if he upset me and excuses himself abruptly. It's as if he only sees me as the victim. That escalated into an awkward situation quickly. Maybe he saw me as someone in need of help or emotionally damaged and broken. Or maybe it was because I scared him away with all my emotions.

Doesn't matter, just keep breathing.

In...1...2...3...out...3...2...1...

***

The next few days blur from one right into the next. I know as a nurse we try to keep patients on a routine so that they can maintain it once they get home, but I never thought about it from the patient's point of view. It's absolutely dreadful, and boring.

I'm sick of being told that healing takes time.

There's no rush.

Take it slow.

Don't get up without help.

I swear I hope I don't get on my patients' nerves like this. I just want to scream with frustration at how slow I'm progressing. I know that progression of any kind is good news, but I need to get out of this hospital room. It's depressing, including the flowers dying on my bedside table; they have all dwindled down to wrinkled petals and dried stems.

Knock...knock...

I turn my gaze to the doorway, Brody is standing there all clean and in scrubs. Looks like he didn't hesitate getting back to work. He says it is easier to keep an eye on me with him being back to work. Somehow, I find that hard to believe.

"Hey there beautiful, I'm on a break and thought that I would take you outside for a walk. I got the ok from the doctor to get you out of this room." He stretches into the hallway and wheels in a wheelchair with a big smile on his face.

This man is my hero!

"Yes, please. I need out. I'm starting to get four-wall syndrome here." I eagerly agree and press my call light to get help to get out of bed.

Temporarily setting aside the fact that Brody is a vampire, he dismisses a nurse and effortlessly lifts me out of bed, placing me in the wheelchair, along with a blanket, as if prepared to make a jail break.

Like bandits making an escape, he peeks around corners of hallways, trying to avoid as many people as possible. He knows that I just can't handle people invading my personal space right now. They all want to give condolences and touch my shoulder for support, which helps them feel better. But right now, physical touch triggers my magic and PTSD, causing me to cast magic with an ease that seems unnatural.

I've noticed since becoming a hybrid that I'm more powerful. I don't need to physically say the words to cast, so long as I am thinking about them. Eve says that this would have happened after practicing magic for a few more decades had I not become a hybrid. I feel like she is hiding things from me about what it means to be a hybrid and unlocking my true potential of power, but I know that I'm not ready to even discuss or think about such things right now.

Right now, I need to focus on healing.

And my grief.

I'm so grateful to Brody, for getting me out of that room and for coming back to work so soon. He's been one of my few constants since waking up. I don't know if he even understands how much having lunch with him has kept me sane while trapped in this hospital. Prison is what I call it.

Breaking the silence and my negative headspace, Brody clears his throat. He's managed to get me into the gardens and is holding a styrofoam cup to me. I can smell the delicious, hot dark chocolate before I bring it to my lips. The taste of it coats my tongue and slides down my throat and melts my body from the inside out. A low, slow moan slithers out of me.

Brody just looks over at me and smiles as he takes a seat on the bench next to me. The one thing I enjoy most about Brody's company is that he understands my appreciation for silence, as well as understanding my need to unleash and confide my feelings in him.

"Dr. Perkins says that you'll be ready to go home tomorrow." His statement hits me hard, filling me with many conflicting emotions.

Home.

My home that used to be with Shadow.

I know that I can't go back there just yet. I'm not ready to be on my own 100% of the time. "I don't want to go home just yet," I say softly. Brody nods in response, understanding my fear of being alone in my condition.

He watched the recording of my conversation with Dr. Perkins and the SA therapist from a few days ago. The recording was handed over to the police shortly afterward as my statement in the case. Brody was shown the recording during his interview process with the police. After watching my recording, he came to me and told me of his ordeal. His trauma was hand-delivered by Declan the entire time. Declan didn't just physically torture him; he bled him out to the point of desiccation, would give him blood, and then bleed him out again. The act of desiccation is one of the most painful experiences a vampire can suffer; death would have been easier.

My parents have already called and told me that I wouldn't be going back to my home anyway. And to appease them of their worry over me, I didn't fight when they said that Galen demanded that I would be returning to the pack. Especially now that I'm a hybrid, which makes sense to be around other werewolves during my first shift.

Not quite ready to be around others but understanding that I need to be around the pack, Galen says that he has had a construction crew working round the clock building me my own house on pack territory. Granted it may be my own house, but it's right near the pack's main house. Galen says that it's so that I can be closer to my parents and for security and medical reasons. I think it's because he wants me close for a booty call and to make sure that Brody isn't sneaking through my window late at night.

The thought has me smirking. I know being home will make my parents happy to help me with my recovery. I know I shouldn't complain; I'm grateful for all that they have done, however, all I know is that the sooner I'm out of the hospital, the sooner I can call Eve forward and shift to speed up the healing.

My time outside my room is a reality reprieve. As Brody takes me back inside, we run into Dr. Perkins, who states that she needs to talk to me later and review instructions for my discharge. I nod in agreement; Brody continues to wheel me inside, making polite head nods and smiles at people that we know who are bustling around the halls.

Brody wheels me into my room and within an instant, I see a beautiful new bouquet of flowers placed on my bedside table. The other dead flowers have been cleared away, pity, I was going to save those for a spell later. I point towards the table, not quite ready to go back to bed just yet. Brody wheels me over.

Taking a look at the bouquet, beautiful dark purple flowers with clusters of white tiny flowers. I instantly recognize them as *conium maculatum* and *aconitum napullus*. Hemlock and wolfsbane. I pale slightly and look for a card or something that may have come with them. A small envelope is lying right next to the bouquet, I grab it and stuff it into my robe before Brody takes notice, not wanting to read it in front of anyone.

Brody places me gently back in bed and notifies the nurse that he has returned me. After being scolded by the nurse, he kisses my forehead and leaves, telling me that he will come by before I leave tomorrow. They both leave, chitchatting about other patients on the unit today, must be a light load if he can constantly come to visit me. I push the thought out of my mind, I'm not working, so it doesn't matter.

I wait a few moments until after Brody and the nurse leave before I reach into my pocket and withdraw the small envelope. My hands shaking and my pulse racing with fear and anticipation. Taking a slow deep breath, I withdraw the small note and read it to myself...

You'll always be mine, princess.
Be seeing you.
XX

Oh my god!
It's not possible.
I know Maybelle said that my kidnapper survived the spell, that spell was everything I had in me. I just never thought he would find me again so soon. What the hell? He's out there, my kidnapper.

'Eve, what do we do now?' I ask her, trying my best to stem my fear and anger.

'We wait. We heal. And then we plan to take back our lives, and take back the power of ourselves that he stole from us.' Eve's courage is like a warm shield flowing through my veins. Where Shadow was my Master Yoda, she is definitely Master Qui-Gon Jinn.

I breathe through my trembling; I will not give in to my fear. My heart is racing, pounding in my chest, ears, and head. *Deep breath in...1...2...3...* I will not cry. *And out...1...2...3...* I will be strong.

'I think the best thing to do right now is to call your nurse and ask her for something for the pain. It will put you to sleep for a little bit and then you can wake up to deal with it all later. It's not a solution, but a band-aid, which will have to do for now until we get out of here.' Eve is right, once again and I find myself not fighting her as I hit my call light to get my nurse.

My nurse comes and brings me my pain meds and I drift off to a peaceful rest, even just for a little while. I welcome the darkness that comes with taking my pain meds. I need a moment to pull myself together.

***

I hear voices stirring me awake. I don't want to open my eyes; opening my eyes means having to deal with reality. Right now reality is not my friend. I barely open my eyes to see my parents talking with Dr. Perkins. Most likely discussing every detail of my discharge instructions.

I clear my throat and all three turn towards me. My Mom flies to my side in a flash, grabbing my hands tightly. "Mom, I'm fine. I just needed to rest. I think I over-did it with Brody earlier." I'm practically being smothered by this woman, thank god my pain meds are still working, because she is literally crushing my already broken bones.

Dad sees my discomfort and rushes over, peeling Mom off of me gently. "Darling, let Callie breathe so that we can review all the details with Dr. Perkins and get her home."

As they discuss the details of my recovery, my thoughts drift to Galen, the silent guardian who has stood watch over me throughout my ordeal. I'll be right there on pack territory with him, so close, and yet my feelings towards him have changed.

My feelings toward myself have changed, I can't even look at myself in the mirror yet. I've accepted what happened to me. I've accepted Eve as my wolf and myself being the first hybrid. But the thought of physical touch, let alone in a sexual manner, has me spinning into panic attacks. And now, my kidnapper knows where I am; it's only a matter of time until I'm well and healthy enough to take him on. Next time, he won't get so lucky.

Dr. Perkins is still talking to me and my parents, thankfully she didn't notice that my thoughts drifted. Bringing my attention back to the discussion, my parents ask so many questions making sure that there is nothing uncertain about my recovery. I'll be seeing multiple therapists to help me along, physical therapists, occupational therapists, as well as an S.A. therapist.

The first step in their elaborate plan is to get me out of the hospital and settle into the house that Galen has set up for me. Then the hard work with all the therapists starts, if they only knew that the minute I shift and bring Eve forward so then all my physical wounds would be healed.

Eve and I have agreed that the next full moon will be when I shift. She says that because I'm a hybrid, my shift should be smooth and almost painless. However, the next full moon is still a couple of weeks away. I apparently missed two full moons during my captivity and my coma state. So until then, I have to play the helpless witch with two broken limbs and heal the slow way.

"Callie, do you have any questions?" Dr. Perkins interrupts my thoughts, like popping bubbles.

"When can I leave?" I give her a small smile, it's not that I'm not grateful for everything that the team has helped me with, but I just want out of this place as soon as possible.

Knock...knock...

"Actually, Dr. Perkins called me earlier and said that you could leave. Today in fact." Galen's masculine voice draws my attention to the doorway. He's standing there with a wheelchair in front of me as if he anticipated my need to want to leave.

I smile over to him and nod.

"I'll go print your discharge paperwork, but before I do, I need to have a moment alone with Callie to discuss something she confided in myself and the SA therapist. If you all don't mind excusing us for a moment." Dr. Perkins holds her hand out towards the doorway.

Everyone leaves, my Mom taking my Dad's arm, waving and saying that they will meet us at home; Galen has agreed to take me to my new house. He makes a comment excusing himself, but I can tell that Dr. Perkins isn't convinced that he won't stay within earshot. She walks to the door and shuts it until it clicks tight.

Dr. Perkins comes back to the bed and takes a seat next to me, taking my hand, and attempting to offer me some comfort. She sighs, I can tell that whatever she has to talk about is difficult. "This is hard, I'm sorry, I'm trying to figure out how to tell you this. I've kept it out of your medical record in case employees look in there before we had a chance to talk."

"Dr. Perkins, just tell me. Whatever it is, I can handle it." I assure her, now if only I believed it myself.

I thought I had the capability to handle it; that is until Dr. Perkin's dropped a bombshell of all news. The news of being pregnant is one thing, but the revelation of expecting twins is a complete shock. My brain broke when Dr. Perkins revealed that I'm pregnant and have a rare medical condition where each baby is carried in a separate womb.

Uterus didelphys is when a woman is born with two uteruses instead of just one. This rare anomaly occurs only in about 0.3% of women; Dr. Perkins believes that the reason I never knew was because I lived in pack territory where preventative medical care, like having a yearly PAP smear, is hard to come by. I know I have lived off-pack territory for some time now and I always meant to set myself up with a gynecologist, but life happens. I had always assumed because my cycle was regular that I never had anything to worry about.

The weight of reality sinking in feels like an elephant crushing my chest, with anxiety creeping in and making it hard to breathe. Pregnant. It's a word that evokes a mix of fear, uncertainty, and disbelief. In the midst of my chaotic thoughts, there's a faint spark of something else. Despite shattered expectations, a spark of hope remains.

As Dr. Perkins further explains the rare condition behind my pregnancy — two uteruses, two babies, each one having two different fathers — I feel like my world has been turned upside down. It's like a nightmare come to life, ready to tear apart my world. Continuing with a composed and professional voice, the doctor explains that while the condition is rare, the fact that I'm pregnant makes it even more unusual. The odds of getting pregnant with uterus didelphys are so low, which makes my situation even more remarkable.

Dr. Perkins privately conducted tests on the babies and handed me an envelope with the results, confirming their ages and different fathers. The age proximity of babies is a few days apart makes it difficult to determine the father, considering semen can remain viable in the body for up to 5 days.

Nausea waves within me at the realization that I know who the fathers could potentially be; Galen and my kidnapper. However, Dr. Perkins says that there is no way to be 100% sure until after the babies grow more, then tissue samples can be collected and be tested against the potential fathers.

Dr. Perkins says that it's my choice if I want to keep both babies, however, if I want to abort, then I would have to abort both. She states that there is no way to safely abort just one baby. It's an all-or-nothing decision.

At that moment, realizing the magnitude of what awaits, I understand that I'm making an unprecedented decision. It has the potential to shape my future beyond my wildest imagination. Nevertheless, I am not alone because I have my family and friends who are always there to offer their support, whatever challenges may arise. This must be one of the outcomes that Helios and Selene were trying to get me to understand. I just never assumed that this was even a possibility.

As I piece together the fragments of memory from my imprisonment, my mind spins. One of the babies belongs to Galen, the symbol of our feelings and connection to the nights we shared. The other one, conceived from the deepest depths of my pain, belongs to the masked attacker who violated me. It's impossible for me to pick one baby over another.

Confronted with a shocking revelation, I find myself at a critical juncture, with a daunting decision ahead that will profoundly impact my future.

Sitting in silence, I feel crushed by the doctor's words, suffocated by their heavy weight. A whirlwind of conflicting thoughts and emotions battle for control within my mind.

Knock...knock...

The door opens and Dr. Perkins excuses herself. Galen comes forward, wheelchair in tow, "Are you ready to get out of here?"

I simply nod to him and smile weakly, too speechless with the bombshell of information swirling around in my head.

'Eve, I know what I'm going to do...'

Epilogue

Masked Assailant

H E IS SO PREDICTABLE, Galen, coming to her rescue like that. His only mistake was getting involved with her, to begin with, with Callie. If he had just left her alone, none of this would have happened. Pacing back and forth among the rubble of what's left of my room in the Old Hospital in the Warehouse District.

I need to come up with a new plan...

Actually, that's not true, not completely. They BOTH needed to stay away from her. I've wanted her for so long, spent so much time building her trust, and finally, I had her all to myself. So, it may not have been the way I had envisioned, but she was mine.

She will be mine again...

Even if I have to kill them all; I would do it too, kill them all, for her...

But he didn't come alone, oh no, he had to bring her familiar. The beast alone was hard enough to gain his trust. It's most unfortunate that I had to kill him. I truly didn't want to do it, but then seeing the pain on her face as my dagger withdrew from him, dripping with his blood, filled me up with enough satisfaction that I lost this battle for her. I was quite surprised by his action to attack me head-on, he must have known that he was dying for her. There is just no other explanation as to why he would attack.

Cleaning the blade with a cloth, leaving no trace of the beast's blood on it has taken me hours. The last thing I need is for her to perform any spells or magic and have her realize that it was me all along. Or for her to come find me, not that she is going to be ready for that anytime soon, not with her injuries.

I wonder what Galen thought of my handiwork on her back...

I'm not sure what brought me more satisfaction, my blade slicing up her back while using my whip or my dagger killing her familiar and sending her over the edge to blow up the building.

Her losing her familiar will make her vulnerable, just barely though, she has no idea how strong she truly is. I don't think she truly understands that her power, her magic, is limitless. She endured days of torture and rape by my hands alone, she can endure this pain and heal from this. It's just going to take her time. She will need someone she trusts to talk to, to help her figure out what to do next. I'll be that person for her, just as I have been for years.

Packing up what's left of my belongings into a suitcase, the building isn't safe anymore, not since Callie unleashed all that magic. I'll need to bring everything back to my apartment, but after I clean it all first. I'll need to perform some protective magic on my apartment too. The last thing I need is for her to figure out that I'm her kidnapper before I'm ready.

I need to plan my revenge against Galen carefully.

Or better yet, I need to plan to swoop in and become the one that she needs and only needs. Heading back to my car, I pass several vampires that are picking through the rubble around, trying to find anything of value to take with them.

Callie's spell certainly shattered plans that the Queen and I had, but no matter, we will persevere. Elona may have gone into hiding with Declan, but I know that she will reach out to me when it is safe. Once the chaos of uncertainty has settled and life has started to go back to normal I'm sure that she and I will resume our drug trials again.

Until then, I'll be going back to my life as if nothing has happened. The radio crackles through my thoughts.

"Officer Monroe, do you copy?"

Picking up the responder, "Officer Monroe here, loud and clear."

Acknowledgment

Having a dream like writing a book was completely out of my comfort zone. There are a few people in my life constantly who help me stay sane and focused on my dream and encourage me to make it a reality. My husband Chris and my Nana. Now if Grampy were still with us today, he would be in my corner with Nana giving me strength and praise on a job well done. I know that this is making him proud wherever he is.

I'd like to thank Geri B. for all the help with the revisions and ideas. I'm sure I've been a handful, but I truly appreciate her always being there for me to help keep me focused and dedicated to my dream. No words can truly say how thankful I am or express how much joy it is to have lived my dream.

To all those who backed my Kickstarter, my words are at a loss for how much I appreciate your support. I was shocked when I became fully funded; I had made so many mistakes along the way to create one, but after 32 generous backers, I was able to raise the funds needed to help publish this book. My hope is that when I launch another Kickstarter that my backers will grow. I just want to thank you all; The Creative Fund by BackerKit, Leslie, Amanda E., Daleina, Mike A., Ashley, Geri B., Kayla H., Stacey P., Simon K., Cara B., Maryly S-S., Sara, Alexis B., Chelsey, Flori R., Katie A., McKenzie C., Chris S., Carolyn R., Cammie M., Janice W., Daniel B., Karen R., AJR Smith, Susan

B., Marsha R., Ashley, Alexandra C., Tamika, Doreen S., Maria, Danial A-H., and Stephen K.

About the Author

M. A. Ramsay-Scales

Once upon a time, there was a girl, who had learned many life lessons and became a woman... That is a story for another day. Thank you for purchasing my book; your support truly means the world to me. I hope that you find as much enjoyment in reading this fictitious work of art as I did in writing it. This book has always been a dream of mine and I hope that after you read it you can understand how important this book is to me.

Apart from being a writer and avid reader, here's a little bit about me. I have found my real-life Alpha, we are happily married, and raising/loving two children. I enjoy finding joy in the farm life surrounded by bunnies, chickens, sheep, and a protective dog.

Alongside my other responsibilities, I work as a nurse in an outpatient hematology-oncology clinic. I have many loves and I'm so glad to share this passion with you.